VOYAGERS

VOYAGERS

short stories by

RUSS DESAULNIER

LUMINARE PRESS
WWW.LUMINAREPRESS.COM

This collection is a work of fiction. Although some stories were inspired by the author's recollections, all are finally and wholly products of his imagination. Resemblances to people, living or dead, apart from the few mentioned public figures, are purely coincidental and unintended.

VOYAGERS
Copyright © 2023 by Russ Desaulnier

All rights reserved. This book or any portion thereof may not be reproduced or used in any manner whatsoever without the express written permission of the publisher, except for the use of brief quotations in a book review.

Printed in the United States of America

Luminare Press
442 Charnelton St.
Eugene, OR 97401
www.luminarepress.com

LCCN: 2023919404
ISBN: 979-8-88679-398-7

For
Bonnie

"The real voyage of discovery consists not in seeking new landscapes, but in having new eyes."

—MARCEL PROUST

CONTENTS

Voyagers 1

The Fisherman 13

Old Larry 24

Rub Story 34

My Father's Footsteps 46

On the Road 56

Grandma 68

Nogales 78

Two Gentlemen of Sedona 88

Sumo 99

Eliot and Esther 108

The Cowgirl and the Mafioso 121

Long Ago and Far Out 132

The One-Eyed Girl 145

Voyagers

It was like having had too much to drink. My head was woozy, and I kept feeling the urge to retch. If only my stomach would stop churning. The steady cold breeze from the ocean brought some relief, so I wrapped myself in a deck chair blanket and got myself comfortable and breathed deeply, my first relief. I couldn't stand to be in my claustrophobic tourist class cubicle in the bowels of the ship. In the wind-blown salt air, my head began to feel clear, and I was able to doze off as the ship swayed and dipped in the rough seas. It hadn't been a good beginning to the voyage.

The SS Constitution was a 24,000-ton ocean liner from New York in route to Gibraltar and the Mediterranean on which I had a round trip tourist class berth as a gift from my father for having successfully completed my first year of college at Cal State San Diego. I was to get a hundred dollars a month remittance for living expenses for six months. Spain was a bargain in those days. Once the ship dropped anchor, I'd ferry to Algeciras at the southern tip of Spain and take a train to Madrid.

My father had been adventurous in his youth, a Depression era tent boxer, a Newfoundland Cod fisherman and a paratrooper in France during WWII, and he'd retained a romantic streak, sometimes reciting lines from Byron, Shelley and Keats. He had indeed survived and prevailed over a lot of hard knocks, and he wanted me his only child to have everything, including my dreams. He must have believed in my ability to take care of myself because he knew why I wanted to go to Spain but he didn't drag me into that discussion. I'm sure he over-ruled my mother's objections, or there wouldn't have been any voyage to Spain. He did tell me, however, to use discretion and not overstep my abilities or knowledge. *Don't bite off more than you can chew.* He'd raised me to be sensible, and he knew it. *And don't forget, you have your education to complete.*

He'd once come down to Tijuana by himself on a Sunday during my recent spring break when I'd had one of my amateur border fights in the Charro ring near the Tijuana racetrack. I handled myself well that day in the face of a sizeable young fighting bull. Even though my afternoon hadn't exactly been a triumph, I'd had some good moments, demonstrating my mettle as well as a good measure of art, according to a reporter for the sports section of El Mexicano, the local newspaper.

These days people take cruise liners on calm rivers or around the Caribbean, but few know what it means to cross the Atlantic during stormy seas because they fly. Until I took the voyage across the Atlantic, I had no idea of the awesome immensity of the ocean. I'd only surfed the easy waves at Trestles Beach near San Diego. My steerage-class berth was claustrophobic, the air stale and consisted of a cubicle that felt more like a walk-in closet with only a small porthole for a window that could neither be opened, nor anything seen through it except waves. I learned to escape by staying topside on the decks as much as possible.

The only consolation of my berth was my cabin mate, Enrique Molino, five years older than me who was returning home to Spain. He spoke English fluently and was good company. He had been studying medicine and now he was returning to establish himself in Valencia, his hometown. I told him, of course, about my ambition to become a bullfighter and he told me many young Spaniards started out wanting to become toreros but almost always changed their minds after a few times in the ring with young animals. As luck would have it, Enrique was an aficionado of bullfighting, *La Corrida de Toros*, and he introduced me to the Spanish poet Federico Garcia Lorca and his famous poem *The Death of Ignacio Sanchez Mejias* in a book he'd borrowed from the ship library. Enrique had become an aficionado as a boy when his father took him to the bullfights on Sundays and festival days. When he was ten, he saw the legendary Manolete triumph in the Valencia ring. He told me what a huge national tragedy it was when Manolete was killed by a bull in Linares that same year. Even the famed horn wound surgeon Jimenez Guinea couldn't save the great torero.

Enrique was to become a general practitioner in Valencia once he got licensed. That was his family's wish to which he was bound by honor not only as a Spaniard but because the family had gone without by sending him to America to study. We spent afternoons walking around the decks of the ship from bow to stern. We loved the salt air and shared our dreams in a mix of Spanish and English. After a couple days, I took to calling him Doc and he called me Miguel, the Spanish version of Michael. I believed I was destined to become a matador and didn't see anything wrong in assuming that identity in advance. Enrique was already a doctor, except for his license, but he already knew what to prescribe for an illness and knew how to sew up a wound. The wild expanse of the sea on a ship with a thousand strangers and our shared Spanish dreams bonded us. Both of us met the style of gentlemen of the day with sport coats, white shirts, and slender dark ties during our daily strolls on deck. We both felt important enough to make our way above to the first-class deck and walk about like a couple of peacocks, smiling and nodding to young unaccompanied women.

On our fourth day at sea, now calm, we were taking our usual stroll up on the first-class deck when we came across a family playing shuffleboard, two grown daughters and their middle-aged parents. As we passed by their shuffleboard court, one of the young women shuffled her disk too forcefully—I suspected intentionally. The dashing Doctor Enrique intervened with his foot stopping the advance of the weighted disc heading far beyond the limit of the painted court. The young woman approached us and graciously thanked Enrique. It was obvious to me this young woman and the one that closely hung behind her were anxious for some social contact as much as we were.

"Doctor Enrique Molina, *estoy encantado*," my friend introduced himself with a formal nod to the young woman when she thanked him for rescuing her errant shuffle disc. She was American, blonde, and pretty, and well-spoken. She introduced herself as Maggie and the younger woman, her sister, as Annette. I stepped forward and introduced myself to both girls. The younger one, Annette, smiled approvingly at me and then the girls introduced their parents, who had hung back while the girls broke the ice. The tall, graying father stepped forward, warmly smiling, and offered his hand to me and then to Enrique. The elegant attractive mother took her place with the girls as if she also felt that after four boring days at sea they were thankfully seeing some bright change. They were a wide-eyed, upper middle class American family on their first ocean voyage in route to Italy for a tour, and everything new they encountered was a delight. I guessed that Enrique and I looked just handsome and foreign enough to be of interest, most likely prompted by Enrique's Spanish accent, which piqued their curiosity. Then began the adventure of our ocean crossing. The mother wondered, obviously cued by the girls, if we were engaged for dinner. Of course, we weren't, and we happily agreed to join them at their first-class table that evening where we would be the father's guests.

During that afternoon Enrique and I convened about how we were going to manage this wonderful opportunity to dine in first class, perhaps for the duration of the voyage, if we played our cards right. What story were we going to concoct for the Eversons and their two pretty daughters, Maggie and Annette. They were obviously impressed by Enrique's being a doctor, but what was I but a lowly sophomoric college boy with nothing special to recommend me? Yes, I was a college boy going to Spain with the intent of becoming a bullfighter, but I felt the story had to be embellished to get more than a passing interest if my flirtation with Annette was going to develop. I suggested to Enrique he pose as my manager, *apoderado*, on the side of his medical practice. After all, the famous Dr. Alfonso Gaona in Mexico managed bullfighters as well as being the impresario of the Mexico City Monumental bullring. Enrique, with his surgical skills, would naturally be welcome in taurine circles with his ability to treat horns wounds. I had a handful of good 4X6 black and white photos from my actions along the border to support my torero story. I lent some of the pictures to Enrique to carry in his sport coat over the next several days. Enrique turned out to be a capable and enthusiastic collaborator in my play. He knew the power of his accent and his Tyrone Power good looks, and so, with our story decided, we prepared for our evening dinner with the Eversons.

Enrique and I were thrilled that all went so well. There was no problem entering the first-class dining area, taking two extra seats at the Everson's table and enjoying food that was a cut above what we'd had so far in third class—no prosaic mashed potatoes with hamburger, but instead a tender medium rare piece of steak smothered in rich mushroom gravy with braised spring potatoes and a separate salad plate accompanied by a rich Roquefort dressing. Fortunately, the weather had allowed for some calm seas and settled stomachs so that we could enjoy the delicious change in the dinner menu.

We were seated next to the girls, Maggie the elder conveniently next to Enrique and Annette next to me. The Eversons were from Rhode Island, and I found the girls somewhat different from those I'd known in California. They had a certain polish, charm and frankness that sparkled with subtle hints of flirtation.

"So, what's your major, Michael?" Annette asked, unfolding her napkin and sedately laying it across her lap, her lucid blue eyes probing me.

"I haven't declared yet. I have no idea. When I return, I'll decide."

"I just completed my first year at Boston College and I'm undecided. Next year I might go to Juilliard if I'm accepted," she said, sighing with indifference.

I only knew that Juilliard was an elite music school somewhere back East. Annette was attractive in an aristocratic way, dressed conservatively with nothing overstated. Being only 19, she needed no makeup and wore only pale lipstick and small pearl earrings, and her light brown hair was neatly pulled back and taken up to emphasize her delicate facial features and slightly blushed cheeks.

"Annette is an accomplished classical pianist, aren't you, Darling?" Mrs. Everson piped in.

"Still in process," Annette added modestly, a little embarrassed at her mother's flattery.

"So, what are you planning to do in Spain, young man?" Mr. Everson asked. Fortunately, no one asked about my parents, as if I were a delinquent boy.

"I will be fighting bulls in provincial rings," I said as a matter of fact and thus started the gambit of my embellished pose with Enrique's help.

"Yes, I am going to arrange Miguel's debut in provincial rings near Valencia where I live. Very little money, you understand. He needs more experience. The provincial actions will give him that." Enrique said.

"Isn't that outside your line of work, perhaps contrary?" Mr. Everson injected, raising an eyebrow. He was a man around fifty, fit and forthright, but warm. He had mentioned he was in manufacturing without any further details, but he had to be successful to be able to take his family for a vacation in Italy.

"One of my specialties is traumatic wound surgery," Enrique said, staying on script. "Spain needs more doctors for this difficult specialty. With more than fifteen hundred corridas a year, and many more unrecorded village bullfights, there is a broad need for expert wound surgery. Aside from my being a doctor, I have always been a great aficionado of my country's unique art of bullfighting, and

I decided to help Miguel as his manager while he stays in Spain. As a surgeon specializing in horn wounds, I will have broad contacts and influence in the bullfight world."

Enrique could have also been an actor. He played into our pretense beautifully, and now Annette was looking my way with a coquettish warmth.

"How did you two meet?" Mr. Everson asked.

Enrique sipped his wine and extended his tale.

"I took a vacation to Mexico, the border, and I saw Miguel in a couple novilladas, novice bullfights, and I liked what I saw. Coincidently, I met him at my hotel in Juarez where he and his friends were having a party after the novillada. That was when I introduced myself, congratulated him on his action in the ring that day, and I suggested he should go to Spain where bullfighting is much better developed and seriously managed than in Mexico. We sat and talked over a few drinks, and I offered to help him if he came to Valencia."

Enrique withdrew my photos from his coat pocket and passed them to Mr. Everson. They were good stop-action black and whites from my few actions along the Mexican border. Mr. Everson was impressed and then passed the photos to his wife, who perused them and then passed them to Annette.

"Those horns look pretty sharp," the mother commented.

"Aren't you terrified doing this?" Annette asked.

"Aren't you scared when you give an important piano recital?" I replied.

"Of course."

"Pretty much the same fighting bulls. You jump in and then you're okay. You find what you have to do," I affirmed.

"Yes, but I don't run the chance of requiring Dr. Enrique's services."

"Don't you ever feel it's cruel, Miguel?' Maggie spoke up.
"Are you enjoying your steak? I asked."
"Yes but…?"
"A brave fighting bull is better off than the domestic animal that gets helplessly slaughtered for steaks in an abattoir," I concluded.

"Fighting bulls are a special ancient breed whose nature is aggressive," Enrique intervened. "They are like prize-fighters. They feel little pain during the heat of battle."

With this last assertion by my Spanish *apoderado*, our company became quiet and had little further to say on the subject. We all toasted a final glass of wine that emptied the bottle to a continued happy voyage and friendship.

The evening ended with the Eversons inviting us to join them again for dinner the following evening and Annette invited me for a game of shuffleboard and a stroll around the length of the ship on one of the lower decks the following afternoon. Enrique had asked the older sister Maggie to accompany him for some dancing on an upper level where a combo was playing the following evening, to which her parents nodded approval.

The next day, halfway through a game of shuffleboard, the seas became rough and made the game impossible to continue comfortably, and so Annette and I retired to the chaise lounges, and we covered ourselves with the provided blankets to ward off the quickly dropping temperature and the light spray blowing off the growing turbulence of the sea. It was exhilarating and deeply warming to be snuggling close with a companionable young woman in such an environment, a bit like sleigh riding with a sweetheart and being bundled together against the cold. Most people had cleared the decks and gone inside while a few, like us, hunkered down in the dropping temperature. Tourist cabins like mine and Enrique's were stuffy and claustrophobic and not welcome when one started to feel queasy.

"I've been invited to play the Steinway piano in the cocktail lounge in the first-class bar on deck three tomorrow evening and I'd like you to come. I'm playing a medley of Chopin. Do you like classical music?"

"Some, I recall some of Chopin's stirring, upbeat music."

"That would be his Polonaise, a kind of Polish dance."

"Well, I'm partial to Pasodobles, like the music in Carmen."

"Maybe I'll play a Bizet encore for you tomorrow night. My father volunteered me to give this recital, but I can play a few other things besides Chopin. My father overestimates my talent because I had a thousand lessons growing up. How did you get into bullfighting?"

"I grew up in San Diego, a short hop across the border to Tijuana where I met an old Mexican guy who spoke good English and owned a leather goods shop that catered to tourists. He'd been a well-known Mexican bullfighter in the 1930s nicknamed *El Mago*, The Magician, because he was known for making some impossible passes with the bulls. When he talked about his adventures in the ring, I was spellbound. Then I saw a few Sunday bullfights at the Tijuana bullring, and I was hooked."

"So, he taught you?"

"On weekends for almost a year along with a few local Mexican boys. He taught us out of love for bullfighting. None of us ever had to pay him anything. He was greatly respected, and the Mexican boys always addressed him as Matador."

The story about El Mago was true but the contracts to fight and Enrique being my manager were fantasy and represented what I hoped would happen in Spain, a launched career with novice performances in provincial rings with young bulls.

"University life got a little better this past semester since I joined the Tri Delta sorority and made a bunch of new friends. Boston College's a pretty good school, I guess. But I really hate those big packed lecture halls when some boring professor just drones away and you're trying to take notes."

"What about Juilliard?"

"That's my father's dream. I think I'd feel like an imposter at Juilliard. You have to play like a budding Van Cliburn to get in."

The breeze off the waves had picked up and we had our blankets pulled up around our necks. Our hands had found each other between the chaise lounges as we pondered the waves that appeared almost deck high.

"I'm just not good enough for Julliard. Do you really want to become a bullfighter?"

"You saw my photos."

"What about Dr. Enrique?"

"What about him?"

"Does he really want to manage you? I mean, won't he be busy being a doctor?"

"We're friends and like he said he's a great aficionado of bullfighting and he knows people in the bullfight world, especially around Valencia. He told me the bullfight circle is held closed, especially to foreigners, but he can get me into the inside where he can get me some provincial opportunities."

Our hands clasped tighter as the pitch and roll of the ship increased and then we both stretched and leaned toward each other and lightly kissed.

"If we stay out here, we'll feel a lot better," I said. "It works, believe me. It's better than Dramamine. We can even snooze a bit in these cozy deck chairs."

"I do like it here with you, Miguel," Annette said. She breathed deeply, closed her eyes, and tucked in the blanket around her neck. "I think I'll be okay just staying at Boston College. I'm an okay pianist but I'm no prodigy. I'm not dedicated like you are to your bullfighting. I haven't found my thing yet."

"I like your honesty," I said and gave her hand a gentle squeeze.

The Fisherman

She kept waving goodbye from the dock until the boat was so far offshore, she was just a tiny figure in her summer kaftan seen from the boat's stern. Jake watched the long white wake pointing back at the dock and Monique. The Pacific was calm as the fishing boat headed out to sea. His pal Barney had assured him this would be a good way to get a quick bundle of cash. For sure, the cool fresh smell of the salt air beat the hot sweaty work of his last job on the high desert construction road gang where he had spent two of the toughest months of his life, his hands getting raw despite gloves. Maybe he'd only be gone a few days this time, and Monique would be glad to see him when he returned with a pocketful of money and a cooler full of Albacore.

The fact was that Jake knew nothing about fishing, except for bass fishing up in Canada when he was a teenager. When he signed up for this job, he wasn't thinking of his ten days on a steamer from Marseille to New York when he was twenty-three and the week of debilitating seasickness he'd suffered. He was only thinking of a $500 stake he could earn if the fishing was good. Captain Jack Bowers didn't ask him a lot of questions. Jake was tanned and fit from his stine on the high desert road gang, physically impressing the skipper he could do the job. One of his duties would be just whipping up some quick food, usually nothing more complicated than eggs and canned beans. He would help Bowers with the jig lines and haul in the fish, gaff them when necessary and toss them into the open hold full of ice.

By late afternoon, they were fifty miles off the coastal town of Laguna Beach. Captain Bowers had some trolling lines out but there had been no activity. They'd pulled in a few Bonito, Mackerel, and Barracuda but no Albacore. Captain Jack was working the jigs and he'd put Jake at the helm holding the speed at 7 knots going due south by the compass toward waters off Mexico. Captain Bowers had shown Jake how to read the compass. It was simply a question of holding the wheel and the boat on a steady course. When nightfall came, Bowers prepped jig lines while Jake heated up cans of beef stew on a Coleman stove for the evening meal. After dinner, Bowers told Jake to join him down on the deck to man the lines. If they hit a school of fish, they'd get busy. Bowers put the boat on auto pilot and gave Jake a slicker to put on and a pair of rubber gloves with rough surfaces for grasping taut lines and slippery fish.

It was about 2 am when they had a flurry of activity with a school, and he and Captain Bowers started pulling in Albacore. Jake got too zealous with a twenty pounder that jumped as he pulled on the line and as the fish jumped upward to the gunnel, it flew high and its tail whacked Jake across the face. Bowers warned him to be steady with the lines and not make big jerking pulls and to watch the water for the fishes' point of exit. It turned out to be a small school and they caught only two dozen fish and the jigs went quiet again. It was about 3:30 am and Jake, despite the activity, was now feeling sick from the ceaseless undulation of the boat. Captain Bowers told him to go up to the cabin and lie down for a spell. Jake's stomach was rolling around and his head was heavy with exhaustion. It was daylight when he was awakened by Captain Bowers. The boat was still because they had docked in San Diego.

"Sorry, Jake, this is where you get off. The fishing isn't too good right now and I don't think you're up to being at sea," Bowers said.

"I can't argue with that, Captain Bowers." Jake was happy to get off the boat, even though he'd have to find his way back to Long Beach."

"Just brought in enough Albacore to pay for expenses this trip, but here's a twenty to help you get back. I'd try something else to make a living if I were you."

Jake thanked the good Captain and went up the dock past a line of fishing boats and up a gangway onto land which he was glad for, but he wondered how to get downtown to the Greyhound bus station. He got directions from a local and fortunately the bus station was only six blocks away from Harbor Drive. With stops, the bus would take two hours and the cost was only $10. It was still too early for the 10 o'clock bus to Long Beach, so he went to a nearby diner and had breakfast and lots of coffee. He could call Monique, but he decided it would be better to get back to his own place and call her tomorrow.

It was good to get back to his apartment without something moving under his feet, no boat or bus. He just chalked it all up to another experience. After he got out of his musty clothes of the last two days, he washed away any lingering regrets with a long shower. Captain Bowers was a decent man. It was hard for Jake to understand how fishermen could ply the seas year in and year out to make a living. Perhaps worse off were those baked guys on the desert construction gang where he'd spent a back breaking eight weeks. Their lives of drudgery were rounded out by nightly beer drinking in skuzzy desert bars. He'd take a close shave and get on some fresh clothes and then pop over to see Monique rather than give her a call.

Sometime he'd have to ask her about her name. Why the French pseudonym? He'd once caught a glimpse of a piece of her mail addressed to Mary Abernathy. Monique was a beauty, but did she imagine herself as some kind of continental siren in the company of Claudia Cardinale and Brigitte Bardot? It was a small thing, so he let it go. Besides, he was used to calling her Monique. Mary just didn't fit her.

He'd been with Monique for almost a year but neither of them broached the topic of their living together. It was apparent that she loved her independence as much as Jake loved his. They were equal and separate, and the balance was stable. Jake had flirted here and there with other women but not taken any of it further. Monique appeared happy with their arrangement, and she was always there for him. What more could he ask for? She taught social studies and history at Wilson Middle School, which was the center of her life from which all else followed. By comparison, Jake's life was in flux. He was her *Tramp Shining*, the poetic figure posed by the Irish actor Richard Harris on his famous hit album of songs which she loved. She could be romantic, but her existence was ordered by her professional life at school. Jake was always impressed that she gave him a corner of her life. Come the summer and her vacation from school, she suggested they go off on some adventure to Oaxaca, Mexico or slowly make their way down the Loire River, staying at hostels. He had no obligations and would have loved to commit to one of her adventures, but he also had no steady money. He wasn't the kind of man who would suggest she pick up the tab for his share of a holiday.

Jake decided he'd arrive at her place when she got home from her day at school, usually around 4 pm. He usually pulled into the driveway of her garage apartment, but not today. She'd hear him coming and his surprise return would be anti-climactic. He parked a few houses down the street, and he'd walk to her door. It was 4:15 pm. When he was about to get out of his old Ford truck, he saw someone pull up in a new red Camaro at the front house of Monique's garage apartment. A polished, grey suited man in his forties got out of the Camaro and started up Monique's driveway. Jake's imagination was immediately piqued toward the wildest and worst suspicions. He sat in his car and wrestled with his thoughts for several minutes and decided to wait fifteen minutes before making his appearance to allow enough time for Monique's imagined infidelity to commence, if indeed that was the case. When he finally left his car for her door, even deep breathing wouldn't slow his heart. He clenched his jaw and fists.

Monique answered her door and Jake could see the blood drain from her face. He'd arrived at a time that required some explaining. She stepped forward, kissed him perfunctorily and stepped back.

"Come in, come in." she commanded as if to allay any suspicion. Jake looked at the handsome Camaro man sitting on her living room couch who smiled and rose to greet him.

"Allan Levin, Monique's principal at Wilson Middle School." He said, offering his hand. "You're the fisherman. Monique told me all about you."

"Retired fisherman, I'm afraid. I found I'm not cut out for the sea." He wanted to ask the principal what brought him to a teacher's home, but he'd wait to see how the situation played out.

"I just made some fresh coffee, Jake. Would you..."

"No, I'm fine."

Jake and the principal were now quiet, acknowledging it was Monique's turn to disarm the situation with some sort of explanation. But the Camaro man intervened.

"They're repainting our administrative offices and we've had a sudden unexpected surge of special needs kids being mainstreamed by the district. It's required some emergency changes and conferencing. Monique was among those whose classes bore the brunt of the surge in new enrollments."

"The discipline problems started on day one," Monique said, showing fluster.

"Some of these kids are on the spectrum." the principal said.

"What's that?" Jake was suddenly lost by the principal's description.

"Kids with mild autistic issues," he added.

Jake had heard about this condition but knew very little about it, other than they were people who acted oddly by a quirk of birth and didn't easily fit into normal society.

"I think I'll be running along and leave you two," the principal said, rising and moving toward the door.

"Monique, as soon as we have a definitive plan for these kids, I'll be seeing you and the others about classroom assignments."

After Monique closed the door behind the principal, she came to Jake.

"Come here, you," she purred and wrapped herself around him and gave him a deep welcoming kiss. "So, what happened at sea, Sweetie? I didn't expect you until Tuesday."

"Apparently not."

"What does that mean, *apparently*?"

"I didn't know principals visited their teachers' homes these days."

"He's making the rounds."

"He couldn't conference everybody at school?"

"Look, Jake, spare me your suspicions."

"This is the fishiest thing I've encountered since I was at sea."

"Very funny. You haven't a clue what's going on at my school."

"So, clue me in."

"The district gave us a day's notice and then dumped a bunch of special needs kids on us. So, what happened to you?"

"I got too seasick to function."

"That's what I mean. Sometimes the unexpected happens. I just don't see mainstreaming these kids."

"Sorry."

"I'm sorry you had to come by at an awkward time."

For the moment, all was settled and well. He spent the night at Monique's apartment and left with her when she left for school the following morning. Jake had business to conduct like getting another job. After cleaning up at his own apartment, he drove down to Ace Hardware on Anaheim Street that had been running an ad in the Press Telegram. In route he decided to swing by Wilson Middle School. At the main entrance there were several vans with company logos, and he saw a worker in paint smeared overalls come out to the trucks. On further investigation, he saw a sign in front that read *temporarily closed, use side entrance*. Okay, it was being painted and fixed up. It was an old school, but it still seemed odd to Jake that a principal would make a business visit to a teacher's home.

It wasn't difficult getting a job at Ace. Thirty hours a week was still part time and so they didn't have to pay any benefits. It had become a growing custom for all kinds of businesses to hire part-time workers and keep costs down.

Who was Jake to question? He'd questioned and marched against the war for five years, but it got prolonged to a bitter end and the fall of Saigon.

It was dawning on Jake that he had to break from just being a working stiff and move himself up on the social and professional ladder. After all, he wouldn't mind a well-fitted Johnny Carson suit and a new Camaro like the principal's. He wondered how much Monique really respected the fact that he was just an itinerant worker. She seemed to have simple tastes and so there was no pressure to wine and dine her. And she loved going out in his old 50s truck. He was her Studs Terkel working class hero, Monique had once said.

Jake decided he'd fix up his place and make it more attractive for them to have more meals there and fewer at her place. He could be domestic. He made great stir fries. He already had a great Marantz sound system and a broad library of LPs and even reel to reel tapes. Good sound was the luxury he'd afforded himself over recent years.

Apparently, the mainstreaming of special-needs kids got winnowed down to a dozen high functioning kids who might make it, and they were spread across all the fourth and fifth grade classes on a trial basis so that no teacher got more than one of the special-needs kids in each class. Monique was relieved and the whole incident with the principal faded into the past.

Jake was a liberal arts graduate of the local college, but he'd never gotten into an entry level position in a business or profession. A lot of his old college friends had gone into government jobs such as social workers, parole officers, even postal carriers. The rest went into the Peace Corps or just hung around town like he did, maintaining but not accounting for the years that were ticking by. Where would one end up at that rate? A few had gone into teaching, but Jake never had much patience for kids and had decided he didn't want to deal with them daily. He had to admire Monique for her patience. Wasn't patience the reason why most elementary teachers were women?

Observing the assortment of people who came through Ace Hardware, Jake learned that a short step up to professional status was in the real estate business. The point was especially made clear when Danny Cook, an old high school classmate, came through Ace to make an order for paint to redecorate a duplex. As a real estate broker, he'd bought the property, was going to fix it up and *flip* it—that is, sell it for a quick profit. He was dressed in a well-fitted suit and was clean cut, usually a mark of higher socio-economic status, higher than Jake's, anyway.

The real estate license course would take two months to complete at City College and cost seventy-five dollars. Taught in the evenings, the course could be easily squeezed into his schedule. One thing about Jake was that when he decided to do something, he went for it like a lion. His problem had always been deciding what to do. The promise of real estate had given him a vision, and nothing would stop him.

Monique encouraged him but said she missed the old Ford truck which he had replaced with a Chevy sedan. He had also bought two suits on sale at Sears and got his hair cut short to match. A new man. He was still working at Ace for a cash stream while working for the Century 21 Real

Estate office on Broadway a few blocks from the beach. Within a month, he had two sale listings on the East side. Jake felt like he'd finally awakened from a long slumber over the past six years since graduation from Long Beach State.

Upon receiving his first sales commission, Jake took Monique to the Northwood Inn on Second Street in Belmont Shore. It was the first time they'd ever been out to a fancy restaurant. The Northwood with its ersatz snow-capped roof was a landmark of Belmont Shore and the place to go for a pricey grilled steak, a cocktail, and a romantic Friday night. Monique had dressed for the occasion in a spaghetti-strapped black dress that focused her slimness. Jake felt weak with love. After dinner, He took her back to his place which he'd cleaned up somewhat and they spent the night.

Three months later, Jake was working full-time in real estate. Ace Hardware and the real estate course were just memories. He was out trying to make sale listings and knocking on doors when he wasn't at the office fielding inquiries or sitting open houses for sale by his office. Summer was approaching and business was good. He saw Monique a little less but that was to be expected. He was now a professional businessman and Monique was busy as ever with her teaching at Wilson Middle School. He had to stay with the job through the summer while the market was hot. He'd have to forgo any trips to Oaxaca or the Loire River Valley. But there was no stopping Monique. She had always been as independent as he was. By the end of June, after school had closed for the summer, she was on a plane to Mexico City and from there she'd bus to Oaxaca City. She promised she'd stay in touch with postcards. The Century 21 Real Estate office phones were alive with inquiries, seller listings of properties and curious buyers. The market was sizzling hot that summer. Suddenly, Jake was clear of all his debts and was making good steady money for the first time in his life. The summer passed with hardly any time for the beach and skimboarding that Jake had loved since he was in college.

By the end of August, Jake had been so busy, he hadn't stopped to reflect that he'd not had a postcard from Oaxaca in several weeks. Another week and it would be September and Monique would have to be back to prep for the beginning of school. No doubt she'd be home soon.

A few days later, he decided he'd drop by and see if she were around. Now he had a brand new eight-cylinder, canary yellow, hardtop Pontiac GTO that he'd be proud to show her. As he turned the corner onto Obispo Street where she lived, he caught sight of her getting into an old beat-up truck. Holding the truck door for Monique to get in was a guy around Jake's age with a ponytail, wearing faded jeans, a vest, and cowboy boots.

Old Larry

Cole didn't have a place to stay when he commuted up from San Diego to teach two days a week at Cal State Long Beach. It was arranged for him to stay with old Larry who was one of those friend-of-a-friend circular connections. Cole's girlfriend Sophie introduced him to her retired Long Beach friend Thelma whose old uncle, Larry, lived by himself in a tiny one-bedroom cottage near the college.

"I bet my uncle would love your company for a few nights a week while you're teaching. He's an interesting old guy and company would be good for him," Thelma immediately said when she heard about my situation, as if she had already been looking to find someone.

Old Larry was in his mid-80s, skinny and bald as a cue ball and a chain smoker. His vision wasn't good enough to drive, so a kind neighbor brought him his groceries and other necessities a couple times a week. Thelma thought her old uncle was lonely more than anything. He kept himself occupied by reading with a large magnifying glass and listening to his collection of opera LPs. He ate sparingly, mostly TV dinners and scrambled eggs. Cole didn't think he had much appetite because of all the smoking he did. He couldn't have weighed more than 120 pounds.

Cole's classes were on Tuesday and Thursday mornings, so he had to arrive on Monday evenings from San Diego and sleep at Larry's place through to Thursday and drive back down to San Diego on Thursday about midday after classes. Apart from his classes, Cole spent a lot of time with Larry. Larry's chain smoking didn't bother Cole because he was a smoker himself, and Larry enjoyed offering his hand-rolled smokes to his new roommate. After a month of Larry's hospitality, Sophie told Cole that Thelma had mentioned old Larry was delighted with his new company. Cole was only 32, and Larry's age and circumstances made him wonder how stark it must be to reach such an august age only to lead a spare, solitary existence. But then resilience is all that Cole knew to this point in his life. He didn't especially enjoy the freeway trips between San Diego and Long Beach in his vulnerable little Triumph convertible amidst intimidating semi-trucks. His classes at State constituted his hopeful building of a teaching career, while living in San Diego, a long commute away.

Cole and Sophie had started in Long Beach three years ago, but then she moved to San Diego after she came into an inheritance from a close uncle. It was warmer there and there were more things to do. Most everyone he knew wanted out of Long Beach and the LA area. Cole didn't have the teaching position when Sophie decided to move to San Diego. He was only substitute teaching in the Long Beach High School district which wasn't especially reliable for a steady income, so he followed her to San Diego and lived with her in the cottage she had bought outright with her inheritance. Two months after moving to San Diego, he got notice from Long Beach State that they wanted to hire him. It turned out his senior professor friend had pulled a few strings for him in the English Department. The job could eventually lead to full-time now that he had his MFA. Sophie was happy for him, though not thrilled that he would be driving up and down the coast every week. But he couldn't pass up the opportunity. His Triumph sports car was economical and in good shape and would serve the commuting well. He was considering old friends in Long Beach where he might have been able to crash a couple nights a week when Sophie told him about Thelma and her old uncle.

Staying with old Larry was a blessing, and fun. Cole had always been interested in older folks, especially if they had lived full lives and were open souls like old Larry. Cole was convinced he could learn something. He wanted to know about Larry's life, and it turned out the old man wanted to know about his. Larry liked his Jack Daniel's whisky, and although Cole was mostly a beer drinker, while he was with Larry, he acquired a taste for Larry's whiskey and his hand-rolled cigarettes.

"Hell, I've been rolling my own since the Great War," Larry said.

"Thelma told me you'd fought in France in World War one."

"The last big offensive in the Argonne Forest. I got lucky when there were thousands who didn't."

"When did you retire from the railroad?"

"Almost twenty years ago now. The Union Pacific is one of the few companies that still has a solid pension system unless you work for the government."

While Cole stayed with Larry, he contributed by bringing in groceries, and he'd cook to give the old man a break which he appreciated. Cole had a comfortable cot and space just off the kitchen by a window that looked out into the small backyard. Larry had a single-sized bed in his tiny bare bedroom that was decorated solely with a framed print of Picasso's *Guernica*. Adjoining the kitchen area was a 50s style chrome dinette set that also served as a desk and catch all. They ate a lot of easy meals like scrambled eggs, hamburgers, spaghetti, and stews made in a crock pot. Larry had a portable TV set on a chest of drawers near the chrome dinette, close enough for him to watch with another pair of thick glasses. Thelma stopped by periodically to see how they were doing. She cared a lot for the old man.

Cole's classes were four sections of Modern American Literature 201, so he could prepare one lecture and do it four times. Not too hard. He knew how most of the lower division kids were under a lot of pressure, so he assigned only a typed 500-word composition once every two weeks with pop quizzes in between to keep the students on their toes. For each paper they could choose a different book from an author on the syllabus which was not discussed in class and write an essay review. He would read or give them a variety of Xeroxed book reviews from popular journals to give them a sense of the ways one could tackle reviewing a novel. He was always on the lookout for brief magazine reviews that demonstrated a different but clear discussion of a book. His workload only got heavy when he had to grade the student book reviews. He was a liberal grader unless a student's work was obviously sloppy and didn't show much thought and effort. A department colleague and acquaintance, Ira Goldman, had his kids turn in self-addressed post cards with the grade they thought they should get. Cole had heard that in very few exceptions that was the grade they were given for the course. He guessed that Ira believed his students knew what they deserved and would be honest about it. He concluded that Goldman could chance experimenting as a tenured professor whereas Cole as a part-timer was always under scrutiny and his position provisional.

Back in San Diego, Cole and Sophie were not getting on, in and out of bed. The nuances of their connection were evading him. He was growing a little ambivalent despite a deep, inexplicable attachment to her. When he was in a mood for love, she wasn't and vice versa. Their timing was off. The good moments were becoming fewer, and he was trying less, as was Sophie. They agreed that when summer arrived, and Cole didn't have to leave town for Long Beach, they would get to the beach more often, have some park picnics and perhaps take a weekend in Tijuana and another in Ensenada.

Because of old Larry, Cole was becoming interested in the theater. Larry was a grand theater buff but his inability to drive had kept him away. So, he offered to buy tickets to some premier theater events if Cole drove them up to the theaters in Los Angeles, a fair offer. This was a luxury Cole hadn't been able to afford, great stage plays with famous actors. Within a couple months, he and Larry with his theater binoculars saw some great shows from premium seats, including *Moon for the Misbegotten* with Jason Robards and Colleen Dewhurst, *Equus* with Richard Burton and Peter Firth and *Streetcar Named Desire* with Faye Dunaway and Jon Voight. Cole was spellbound and got the wild inspiration he'd find a way to the stage. This theater tangent would eventually stretch the cord thinner that held Sophie and him together. Back in San Diego, he had begun spending part of his free time at the Hillcrest Community Theater, volunteering for stage crew, helping with sets and props, and in general getting to know theater from the ground floor up. He was making connections within and biding his time until he could audition for the right play at the right time. His theater involvement grew while he was still commuting to Long Beach and camping with old Larry.

While driving back home from the Ahmanson Theater in Los Angeles where they had just seen *Streetcar Named Desire*, Larry was all excited, more than Cole had seen him since he'd been staying with him.

"Man, the sparks really flew between Voight and Dunaway. But, you know, her lying and trying to be something she wasn't fueled the flame. What do you think?" Larry said.

Cole had been thinking about the sexually charged conflicts in the play that then segued to thoughts of Sophie, how he didn't know how to read her sometimes, how he felt desire and resentment mixed sometimes, not fully at peace with her or himself.

"The sexual tension was intensely powerful. Jon Voight was a convincing Kowalski and Faye Dunaway was a gorgeous, vulnerable Blanche," Cole replied.

Cole felt his response was prosaic, considering he was supposed to be articulate with explications as a literature teacher. The subject of sexuality remained a mystery in his own life. Sexual tension percolated below the surface of his life and held a certain ambiguity as it did in the Williams play. Cole was certainly no Stanley Kowalski.

"You don't talk much about your lady, Thelma's young friend in San Diego. How's that going, Cole?" Larry queried.

"Fine," he said, knowing such a clipped response would put an end to the discussion. Talking about Sophie would open a topic that was too sensitive and difficult to explain.

"I see," Larry said, looking straight ahead out the windshield and he went quiet for the duration of the trip home.

The next morning, Cole was up early, showered and dressed and reviewed his notes for class. Larry shuffled in from his bedroom, not looking well.

"How about some coffee, lots of milk and sugar," he said. He was still in his robe and pajamas and rubbing his eyes. Cole poured him a cup of coffee and started scrambling enough eggs for both.

"Once in a while I get nightmares about the war. It's like reliving it all and it's awful. More than fifty years ago now and I still have the same nightmares, trenches with oozing bodies without limbs or heads. I've heard other vets have similar nightmares. It's a good thing you escaped Vietnam, Cole. War ruins those it doesn't kill." Larry looked exhausted.

Larry sipped his coffee and then began rolling a cigarette. Cole finished his eggs and toast with Larry and then began pulling things together to go out the door for his first class.

"Let's have a nice dinner tonight to celebrate life, a bottle of wine and some steaks. Would you stop at the store for us?" Larry asked, drawing a twenty-dollar bill from his wallet on the table. I've enjoyed our theater outings enormously, and your company. By the way, if your girl in Dan Diego is giving you a hard time, just move on, young man. *Carpe diem*, right? Now, get going or you'll be late for your class."

While driving on Seventh Street toward the college, Cole started to feel sorry that soon when the semester ended, he'd be leaving old Larry to return to his life in San

Diego. Cole felt bad about having to leave the old doughboy. He would have to stay in touch or even come up for an occasional visit.

It was a Wednesday night and they worked on a fresh bottle of Jack Daniels as old Larry regaled Cole over dinner with stories about his life in Chicago in the twenties, about the Chicago Bears, jazz concerts, opera, Jack Dempsey, Prohibition speakeasies and gangsters. The old man became animated as the stories spilled from him. It was almost 11:30 when they decided to turn in.

Cole hadn't missed a class in four semesters, but that Thursday morning would have to be an exception. He called in sick to the English Department office and cancelled his 9 and 10 o'clock classes. Larry was sympathetic and offered to make him some breakfast, but Cole declined and managed to get down some buttered well-done toast and two cups of black coffee with two Excedrin. He decided he'd get an early start and hit the 405 at 10 am when traffic had eased going south. He'd open the windows on the Triumph and let the draft refresh him during the drive down which would get him home several hours earlier than usual.

Sophie's house was a quaint little stucco cottage with a Spanish red tiled roof in a hilly part of the Hillcrest district with a view of part of the city. She had purchased the place outright for $60,000 with some of her uncle's inheritance money. Cole had moved her stuff down from Long Beach for her with a rented truck and then moved himself down a month later.

He didn't see her old Saab when he pulled up in front around 11:30 am. Maybe the temperamental Saab was in the repair shop again or she was out shopping, which was quite possible since he was three hours earlier than his usual arrival on Thursdays. He had a key, so he'd go in and wait for her and make himself something to eat and get a glass of juice.

Cole was about to open the door, when the door swung open before he could put the key in the lock and a surprised handsome man about Cole's age and stature appeared at the threshold. Both men were surprised and speechless for a frozen moment. Cole recognized the man as the real estate agent who'd helped Sophie find the house a year ago. Cole's hangover throbbed, his thought calculating in an instant that the agent was a secret lover who was just leaving the house as nonchalantly as though it were his own. In the next insane moment, impulse took over and Cole threw a punch that stopped the man's progress from the door, catching him squarely in the face and sending him reeling backward into the house and landing him on his rear. Cole then recognized his awful rashness and had no idea what he was going do next when he saw the agent spring up and rush at him, bloodied nose, and growling.

"The goddamn boyfriend!" he uttered in recognition and was upon Cole before Cole could marshal a move. Cole flailed at his antagonist who tackled him to the ground where they rolled until the enraged agent came up on top and straddled Cole. He could have pummeled Cole without his putting up much defense, but the agent suddenly got a disgusted look on his face and got off Cole and started to walk away down the path to the street.

"Ah fuck it!" he cursed, his contempt clear to Cole who was still struggling to get to his feet. The whole incident happened in a flash. Of course, Cole felt humiliated and stupid. He was furious with himself that he hadn't hit the agent hard enough so that he stayed down, and secondly that his hangover had perhaps made him weak. Or was that just a convenient excuse? He was aghast at what he'd done. Sucker punching someone in the face without provocation was an ugly act, and pathetic, and he had to concede he got what he deserved. He thought he wouldn't have lashed out had he been in his right mind. After all, the agent was neither threatening nor provocative and no doubt would have preferred to have quietly left. This was Sophie's doing.

 Cole regretted his neglect of Sophie, but more, he felt sorry for himself and ashamed and sorry he and Sophie would have to end in such an awful manner. He wouldn't be able to talk about what had happened when he returned to Larry's place, nor to anyone he knew. He would want to start forgetting the incident as best he could and bury it. But he knew he'd carry the ugly, shameful memory forever like a scar.

Rub Story

When I recollect our time in Japan, I clearly envision our apartment building next to the Tenpaku River, a sleek, narrow structure with only one apartment on each side of an elevator shaft that accommodated the twelve stories. We were on the eighth-floor next door to a widow named Hirano-San. Being up high with nothing around was a relief from the crowded conditions of Japan, despite how the building swayed during frequent tremors and leaked rain during powerful typhoons. We had some happy years there and I had a good job. For a while my wife Ella started to feel about as content as she was ever going to be living in Japan. We knew other American expats whose troubles and stories lent some balance to her grievances about living in that ancient, strange society.

Our Lion's Mansion building was along the banks of the Tenpaku River which much of the year was a shallow trickle of murky water. During typhoons it became a raging torrent, but otherwise the Tenpaku was a poor excuse for a river. Yet downstream a few hundred yards where the river intersected with a main thoroughfare and ran under a bridge, several Carp would sometimes appear where the stream had carved out a few small pools.

Our subway station Hara was at the intersection of the bridge and the main thoroughfare headed downtown.

From Hara Station, I branched to the many different companies across the sprawl of Nagoya to teach English in the evenings, usually returning a bit after nine pm. I'd walk the three blocks along the river to our building where there was a little bar marked by a red lantern hanging in front, and sometimes I would stop there for a few shots of sake. A red-light establishment had a different meaning in Japan. The *akachochin*, meaning *red lantern* in English, usually inscribed with the name of the bar in *kanji*, could be found in neighborhoods everywhere. In Hara, my *akachochin* was run by a widow named Mie-San, perhaps in her mid-sixties, who always wore a plain workaday kimono and wore her hair up in a sort of Gibson hairdo. She shuffled around the tiny establishment like a Geisha, constantly bowing and demurely smiling. The whole place wasn't any bigger than our modest apartment living room back in Los Angeles. Mie-San lived in a cubby at the back of the shop, separated by a door-sized *noren* curtain imprinted with swimming Carp, the ancient symbol of strength, perseverance, love and beauty. There were four low tables where patrons could sit on *tatami* mats and the bar where most preferred to stand and drink and pick at small plates of grilled chicken, tofu, and *edamame*. The place was crowded when there were more than a dozen patrons. In the States we would have called Mie's place *a hole in the wall,* one of many common English idioms that were difficult for my students.

One night I had been out to Toyota City for an enjoyable class with mid-management students and I was feeling good and in a mood for a drink. Mie-San was behind her counter, prepping small-plate orders. To my right at the corner of the counter was a happy looking Japanese man about my age. It was rare to see anyone in public simply smiling. I guessed that their seemingly fixed impassive expressions were a result of a millennium of oppressive culture and unrelenting work. But sake helped. This smiling, broad faced Japanese man approached me, holding his sake cup and a ceramic *tokkuri* sake bottle and offered me a drink. His smile was so sincere, he radiated palpable warmth. I held my tiny cup in the traditional manner with both hands as he poured with both hands. It was a quaint ritual. I thanked him in Japanese.

"You live in Hara, Mr…?" he said in English.

"James," I said and offered my hand, which he shook, and he made a slight bow. The Japanese reflexively bowed.

"Ando Yukichi. You may call me Yuki."

"Call me Jim," I said, and proffered my sake bottle. He held out both hands with his tiny cup as I poured.

From that moment on we became a proverbial Casablanca *beautiful relationship,* like Rick and Inspector Renault. My wife and I were invited into his home and vice-versa, something unheard of in Japan. During those years of our association, I remember only a few occasions when he didn't have his broad smile. We met frequently at Mie's *akachochin* and he helped me and Ella in many ways through the maze of living in Japan, especially when we were faced with important papers that needed translation or the negotiating of an occasional issue with our landlord. We played tennis sometimes on weekends at a rented court outside of the city limits among the rice paddies where he and Mayumi kept a garden of common vegetables. They often gave us a bag of seasonal vegetables, and we introduced them to broccoli and zucchini with envelopes of seeds we brought back after a summer vacation to the States.

Yukichi was a professor of chemistry at the University of Nagoya, and I a math-incompetent English teacher, yet we found much to exchange and talk about. He dug up his dormant store of conversational English from his undergraduate days, and I began learning new Japanese words and phrases rapidly, inspired by friendship.

Yuki delighted in children, especially the little ones. He adored our blonde, curly haired daughter, then only six when he met her. His two sons were already grown up and about to enter college. His apartment building on the other side of the bridge was in a mammoth warren of typical small apartments, and to make life easier for himself and his family, he had purchased the apartment next door and knocked a doorway through the dividing wall.

We rarely saw the sons, who kept to themselves studying in the adjoining apartment except when Ella and I visited Yuki and his wife on a weekend, and they'd emerge to meet their father's foreign guests and join in a meal. Yuki's wife Mayumi was a high school teacher with a sweet disposition who turned out gourmet cuisine from a tiny galley kitchen with a two-burner gas stove. She was just as warm and generous as Yuki, and over the course of our years in Nagoya, she gave Ella several kimonos to take back to the States as souvenirs. She showed Ella how to make *Tempura Soba, Gyudon and Sukiyaki,* dishes we continued making at home many years later. Mayumi also gifted us with some samples of her stained-glass hobby which still grace our home in the states to this day.

Yuki was not a drunk, but he drank every evening, as far as we could tell. My wife liked Yuki as much as I did but she was convinced he was alcoholic. Alcoholism was rife in Japan, but something not acknowledged. I liked a few shots of sake during the week and a glass or two of Bordeaux on the weekends, but I had to keep myself functional for my job and so I drank sparingly. It was customary for Japanese workers everywhere to join in drinking at bars with their colleagues almost every evening after work. Such a constant custom, I believed, could make an alcoholic of an unwary casual drinker.

Neither Yuki nor I had to drive for our home exchanges. We just had a short walk along the Tenpaku River between apartment buildings. We got together for holidays and birthdays, but what I remember most was Thanksgiving. Ella and I found an international emporium close to downtown Nagoya that carried a wide array of popular American foodstuffs, including frozen turkeys of about ten pounds. Yuki and Mayumi had never eaten turkey. So, Ella and I introduced them to the tradition of the Thanksgiving Day turkey dinner with all the trimmings. In the early years we did the dinner at their place because Mayumi had a small oven that could handle a ten-pound turkey. I showed her how to baste the turkey, and I took over the making of the gravy, something that I had perfected over the years, while Ella prepared stuffing. Mayumi laid out a lovely table in their main room with eight settings including places for our daughter and a pleasant woman piano teacher in Yuki's building who spoke a lot of English. A few years later, Yuki helped us find a new gas oven which we had installed, and we began roasting the seasonal turkey in addition to breads and cakes.

"You must drink beer," Yuki enjoined me, as he held out a half liter bottle of Japanese Kirin. I was reminded of my youth's experience in Spain where the custom was drinking *cañas*, small glasses of draft beer equal to a cupful. As an American, I kept tract of my consumption by bottles.

With cupful quantities, I sometimes lost tract. But I let Yuki continue to fill my glass. His warmth was hard to refuse.

"Jim-San, I toast you. Thank you to bring turkey to my life." The whole room cheered.

The mashed-whipped potatoes with gravy were also something new for Yuki and family along with stuffing, all which was met with a round of "good taste" in English from everyone. The Japanese had imitated many American ways but not our food. These days Taco Bell, Kentucky Fried Chicken and MacDonald's can be found everywhere in Japan. During our time in Japan, American fast food was just starting to show up. One saw few fat Japanese, but that may be changing now.

We had many memorable dinners at our place with Yuki and Mayumi. I still smile when I remember the time when we had guests from Los Angeles, Sam Hirasawa and his wife Peggy. They were second generation Japanese Americans originally from Wyoming. Sam had worked in the aerospace industry with my father in Los Angeles and they were also old golfing chums. Sam and Peggy were traveling Japan to visit a few distant relatives on both sides. I couldn't help wondering how that was going to turn out. Neither of them spoke a word of Japanese. But I had learned how goodwill could overcome the barriers of language.

"You look Japanese but speak no Japanese," Yuki said, perplexed and dumbfounded by my friends from Los Angeles. We were amused as were Sam and Peggy. Were we not any different in the US where most Americans were geocentric and had such little conception of the wider world? The Japanese lived in an exclusive island culture that had historically been closed to foreigners, and even in post-war Japan the door had only been opened a crack. Foreigners were still rare curiosities in the early 80s. I explained to Yuki that America was a land of immigrants and had all sorts. I told him dozens of languages were spoken in Los Angeles. He was happy to hear that Japanese was on the list.

In all the time I was in Japan I never had an exchange about World War II and the war in the Pacific. Later, when I had begun working full-time at the Nagoya foreign studies university, I tried to broach the topic, but everyone reacted as if they hadn't heard me. It seemed as if a kind of national amnesia prevailed when it came to their history of militarism from the 1930s to 1945. But when August rolled around, there was always a somber national memorial for Hiroshima with never a mention of Pearl Harbor. Every year there were loud Chinese protests when Japanese dignitaries and officials paid respects at the WWII memorial at Tokyo's Yasukuni shrine that includes 14 convicted Class-A war criminals.

"Japanese soldier do many terrible thing in war," Yukichi said with a grimace during one of our evening meetings at Mie's *akachochin*.

I didn't know how to respond to this remark. It must have been as difficult for him to say what he did as it was for me to respond. Such a delicate topic. My mind went to the highly publicized incident of former English prisoners of war lining the streets of London who turned their backs when the Japanese emperor Hirohito's motorcade came by during his first state visit. The cruelty of the Japanese during the Pacific War was legend. But that didn't compute with my knowledge of Yuki who was a paragon of kindness and warmth. But then neither did WW II German atrocities compute, considering their high culture that had brought us the sublime beauty of Bach, Beethoven and Mozart.

"I am so happy you are my friend," I said in Japanese which was all I could think to say in that moment, and I poured him more sake.

"You are becoming more Japanese, Jim-San."

It was true. Although I still had trouble understanding many things said to me in everyday conversational Japanese, I had acquired a broad ability to make some kind of response in Japanese. I maintained that if I had come to Japan when I was much younger, I would have learned the language with ease. Something in the brain hardened, I believed, making it difficult to learn a foreign language after 40.

After Ella and I returned to the States and settled in Oregon, I invited Yuki and Mayumi to spend a summer holiday with us—most of their expenses I had already decided to pick up. We had bought a spacious house in Eugene, Oregon with a private guest wing where they stayed for ten days. We took them all over, to the beaches and to the forested mountains and lakes. At Sparks Lake, after I had given them a little tutoring on how to paddle and handle a canoe and fitted them with life jackets, I pushed them off from the shore with a shout of *gambatte*, do your best!

They came back after two hours, flushed and excited, having circumnavigated the whole lake. They had never done anything like it before, not even a paddle around a lake in Japan. We got them situated at the Deschutes River Hotel in Bend and met with them for dinner at the hotel restaurant, a fine steak house. I think the Japanese love steak to the point of fetish, perhaps because of a past with so little meat, and because eating premium meat had become a mark of status in the post-war era. Yuki ordered a 22-ounce Porterhouse steak guaranteed for its tenderness. He was not a big man, and none of us, even Mayumi, thought he'd be able to eat such a big meal, but slowly he persevered and ate it all. We had finished our smaller dinners and we watched him go through the final six ounces of his steak, still enjoying every bite. It was good to see him so happy and triumphant that he'd fulfilled a quest to eat a giant steak, a Japanese dream.

Back at the house in Eugene, Yuki was also bent on seeing how much beer he could drink. Since Ella and I had been gone in Japan, a plethora of micro-breweries had sprung up and there were dozens of Belgium, German and English type ales available. Yuki was excited to try them all and started lining up his emptied bottles like trophies along the wall next to our patio. No matter how much he drank, he seemed to remain sober. He was on his first American vacation and was determined that he would have his fill of whatever he desired. After all, he and Mayumi had treated us countless times to feasts of first-class sushi and lots of Mayumi's home cooking from which we learned and still cook wonderful recipes like her grilled *Saba* mackerel and *Kinpira Gobo*, spiced and braised burdock root.

I don't remember my exact words, but I suggested to Yuki that he had a drinking problem, and it could lead to some bad karma. A cloud descended on his broad face and the smile disappeared.

"I am not alcoholic!" he shot back. I could tell he was controlling his anger, the only time I had experienced that from him.

He seemed genuinely insulted, but I didn't take back my remarks, and simply told him I was just worried about him. I guessed that it was no different with alcoholics the world over. Most are in denial about their habit. Some are lucky enough to seek help before their bodies rebel. He was one of those special alcoholics who was happy under its influence and had carefully managed his drinking for years. How else had he taught graduate chemistry at the university for three decades?

Just after I retired from my foreign studies university and came back to the States, Yuki retired from his position at Nagoya University. We had both reached 65 within months of each other. We both saw that age as time to change course. There were other pinnacles to climb while we were still able. We made jokes about being *toshiyore*, tired old gentlemen.

When Ella and I were packing up to get ready to return to the United States, Yuki was visibly sad, but he understood it was time we went back to our American life, and so he was happy for us. Who was he going to be able to beat so easily at tennis, he said. He asked for my Citi Bank account number so that he could give us a small gift—I expected it would be the equivalent of a few hundred dollars, so I made only a modest protest. Gifting in Japan was customary and so his intention was no surprise. As a teacher in Japan where education was held in such high regard, I had been the recipient of countless gifts, from bottles of expensive whisky to packages of pricey gourmet foods. Over the years, Ella and I had acquired their custom of gift-giving. To this day, we never go anywhere or attend special occasions empty handed. We have been gladly generous with close friends and relatives.

I had forgotten about telling Yuki my bank account and routing numbers. So, when we got a bank statement a few months later when we were resettled in Oregon and we saw a deposit of $10,000 in our account deposited from Japan,

I immediately sent him an email acknowledging his generosity and telling him we didn't deserve such a lavish gift.

"You gave me American world I didn't know. "*Arigato gozaimashita,*" thank you very much, he wrote.

For years after, Yuki and I exchanged short emails monthly and I watched his grammar and writing improve. He signed his letters with *Rub*, in self-mockery of the Japanese difficulty pronouncing the L in love. He took to addressing me as *Monjiro* because I often had a toothpick in my mouth like a popular Japanese TV Samurai character. His boys had finished college, were married and already there were two young grandchildren who probably gave Yuki more joy than anything, judging by the many photos he attached to his emails. He'd be posed with the giggling toddlers, one held in each arm, his familiar grin communicating his joy.

Ella and I guessed that alcohol was catching up to him for he had written that he was doing yoga and walking along the Tenpaku River every day for an hour, but still he was feeling tired, truly a *toshiyore*. We guessed the alcohol had finally gotten to his liver because Mayumi wrote a few months after his last letter that he was fatigued and refusing food except for bowls of warm miso soup, surely a symptom of something serious. She signed off by writing, *Yuki sends you Rub.*

Not long after that, according to Mayumi, he lay down in his last two days, refusing food, as if meditating, and quietly passed on. We still keep a large, studio photo of Yukichi, Mayumi and the boys amidst our gallery of memories on the hallway wall of our house.

I had for some time been dissatisfied with the ragged landscaping around our house and so in my 80th year I redid my front yard in the Japanese style of the Kyoto Zen pebble gardens with a sprinkling of well-placed dwarf evergreens and few river boulders. When I had finished the garden, I had a placard made with Japanese Kanji characters to go on the bamboo fence: *The Memorial Ando Yukichi Garden.* We took photos of the garden and placard and sent them to Mayumi who continued to periodically send us lovely greeting cards with traditional Japanese scenes in which she gave us bits of news and always closed with *Rub.*

My Father's Footsteps

"Now make it black as tar, then blonde and sweet with lots of milk and sugar," were Billy Playfair's directions to me for his afternoon tea break. It was one of my duties on the machine shop floor amidst two acres of machines and their operators at the Dunlop factory in the Erdington district of Birmingham, England. Billy operated a milling machine where periodically a forklift driver would unload unfinished casts of steel to be milled. When he had finished with them, the steel castings would then be picked up and carried to another phase of machining. And so it went with the machines and their operators—milling, drilling and lathing. I was accustomed to the smell of machined steel, because my father had been in the machine tool business most of his life and he always had the smell of cut steel when he got home from work when I was a child, and it became a deeply imbedded olfactory memory associated with the warmth and comfort of my father.

    I had acquired a job at Dunlop because of my father. When I arrived in Birmingham in the summer of '63 after touring Europe, I looked up Percy Wescott who twenty years prior had been my father's teammate playing in the English professional baseball league. Percy had continued with baseball, managing the Dunlop company team which played a much-reduced popular spectator sport from its heyday in the 40s. Nevertheless, Dunlop had a schedule that stretched through the summer, and among its opponents was the American Army that still had a sizable force stationed in the country.

I guessed I was a living reappearance of my father when I met Percy at Dunlop because he couldn't do enough for me. He kept looking at me as though I were an apparition. I probably caused a tide of recollections about that era when he and my dad had played baseball around England together for the West Bromwich Tigers. The same response had happened in London when I looked up Ray Casale, another of Dad's pals when he'd first come to London from Canada in the late 30s, looking for work. When I came up and out of London's Finsbury subway station, Ray claimed he knew it was me immediately because of my walk which he said was just like my father's. I already had some idea of Ray's looks because I had seen his photo in the family album many times posed with my dad at Trafalgar Square under one of the huge lion statues. Dad had fond memories of him and wanted me to look him up. I knew why my dad had made such good friends in England as he did everywhere he went. He engaged people, connecting deeply with warmth and sincere interest in their stories. He had only been at the Curtis Wright aircraft plant in Buffalo three years when he was elected by 300 workers to be their AFL-CIO union president.

When Percy found out I could stay in England through the summer until September and the beginning of my college fall term in California, he asked me if I played ball. Not recently, I replied, but I had played some. I grew up playing sandlot ball until I entered high school and then I became more interested in football. When I was younger, kids at the local playground called me "Mighty Mouse" because I was small but threw a good fast ball from the mound and could often get wood on the ball when at bat. And because I was fast, I was good at stealing bases. My father had coached me as a kid, so I had a few recessive skills left that I would have to call on. When Percy then asked if I would be interested in working at Dunlop in the machine shop while also playing for their baseball team, I immediately responded affirmatively to both propositions. I needed the money.

Although I had no applicable skills in a machine shop, he told me not to worry. He said they'd create something for me to do. Percy had been with Dunlop since the end of the war and had senior standing with the union, a powerful organization in the English manufacturing workplace at the time. He took me into an office on the ground floor of the huge Dunlop plant, filled out a form, got me a union card which indicated my work as *maintenance* and then walked me to the clubhouse and ball diamond on the company grounds where he found a uniform and a pair of spikes that fit me.

From where I was staying with my grandma Doris in Perry Barr, it was about a thirty-minute bus ride to the Erdington Dunlop machine works and the athletic facilities. For the first time in my life, I fully realized the kind of environment in which my father had spent much of his working life. The machine shop was filled with a ceaseless loud drone of steel casts being shaved, drilled and shaped. And it was made especially dirty by the amount of oil lubricant that had to be used. No wonder my dad made such an issue of my finishing college and doing something different with my life. When my father was around fifty, he moved up from the shop floor to the company offices where the blueprints were read, assessed and parts scheduled and assigned for machining. With that promotion, he wore sport coats and dress shirts with ties instead of the traditional lab coat, and he never operated a machine again.

My job at Dunlop was sweeping up metal shavings and debris from the work, which was constant, and making tea for the floor machinists. I made the equivalence of about $45 a week which was fine during that summer, giving half to Grandma Doris and using the other half for bus fares and extras. I already had a return flight to Los Angeles, so my only pressure was to stay on the job and prepare myself to play ball. The irony wasn't lost on me, the assumption that I had to be a competent baseball player just because I was an American and my dad had been a star pitcher back in the day when he and Percy had been teammates.

"So, what position do you usually play, son? Can you pitch like your dad did?" Percy asked.

"I wish," I said.

The fact was, I hadn't picked up a baseball since I was in my mid-teens. My dad and I would play catch during my teens when he wanted to have a father-son talk with me about my schoolwork or some mischief I had been up to. The more serious the talk got, the more stuff he put on the ball, throwing crazy curves or he'd steam one at me for emphasis that hurt my hand to catch. It was a happy father/son ritual which California's weather usually permitted year around. My dad kept his arm loose and effective with that ritual all the way up into his sixties. There were times when we were both younger that we'd go to a local playground with a baseball backstop, and he'd bring along a bucket of old baseballs he'd acquired from a batting range, and he gave me some batting practice. I could hit the easy pitches, but when he started zinging, curving, and sinking them, I was lost. He shook his head and smiled. I just didn't have the natural requisite of the eye-body coordination required for connecting with difficult pitching.

"I've usually played shortstop," I replied to Percy's inquiry. My answer was true, but my shortstop days had been with my middle school softball team. My playing hardball was more about my memories of boyhood than any real young adult experience. When Percy took me into Dunlop's field clubhouse and sorted out a uniform and spikes that would fit me, I felt the seriousness of the illusion into which I had dropped myself. But what choice did I have? I needed the job in the machine shop and in a sense, I was defending my father's honor and keeping faith with Percy's nostalgia and fond memory of my father. In any case, I clung to the hope that I could stop grounders as short-stop and could perhaps get some wood on a few pitches to fulfill the expectations that had been thrust upon me.

Percy was missing fingers on his left hand, obviously not the case when he had been actively playing baseball in the 40s. I asked the right fielder Alf Weatherby what had happened to Percy the first time we had an all-team practice on a Saturday. He told me it was just after the war and Percy was serving with the Home Guard and helping clean up bombed neighborhoods when someone touched off an unexploded bomb that scattered shrapnel, a piece of which sheared off part of Percy's hand. The Home Guard man who had accidentally set off the bomb didn't survive.

"I always remember when we played the American Air Force team the summer of '41 up in Leeds," Percy recounted. "You were just a baby then. Your dad was so proud he'd had a son. He named you Monte after England's famous commander during the war. Already there were a lot of Yanks over here getting ready for D-Day. Your dad went the whole nine innings and struck out 12 batters."

"Did you win?"

"No, we lost 2 to 1, but hell, those Yanks were the league champs that year. They pulled a lot of players from the American majors. There was no shame in that loss. We got some big crowds when we played the Yanks."

I had always been athletic and being in my early twenties I could still easily adapt to the baseball situation, calling on my memory bank. I could get into the batter's box as a lefty with a shoulder width stance and take the required step into the ball with the swing. At shortstop I had the speed to get myself into a crouch in front of the ball and spring into position for the throw to first base. Throwing was the easiest part of the maneuver. But my results were less than modest in our first game against the Nottingham Lions. I had thought and hoped the British lads wouldn't be anywhere near the skill level found back in the States where many kids on high school teams were professional prospects. I threw out a couple hitters who hit easy grounders my way, but I had only one hit because I outran the fumbling response of a third baseman to whom I'd hit a grounder. Otherwise, I fanned four times at bat, took two walks, and got one hit which flew out to right field. I was shocked at the speed the English pitcher was throwing the ball. I didn't even swing at half the strikes that were thrown. Thankfully, we pulled off a win at 6 to 5 over nine innings.

Grandma Doris had been a nurse, retired from Birmingham General Hospital, where I was born. My grandfather Jack had passed five years prior to my arrival—according to Doris because of his life-long smoking of Woodbines, a popular brand of strong filterless cigarette. My mom had written to Doris and asked if I could visit her in Birmingham, and so when I showed up, she not only welcomed me but insisted I stay for as long as I needed. I might have used my return flight back to LA had she not opened her door and her heart to me. Where else was I going to go?

I regret to this day that I was a typical young man of 22, mainly self-absorbed. Looking back, I now understand how caring Grandma Doris was toward me. Every morning she'd have some breakfast ready for me and got me off to my job at Dunlop. And she'd have some dinner when I got back after a day's work. Like Percy and Casale in London, she seemed to be in a reverie about me because I looked so much like my dad who had married her daughter, my mom. But I did at least spend more than half my evenings with her that summer, watching the tele or just chatting. But being young and restless, I got out on the other evenings and went to the Perry Barr Greyhound racetrack or went out with my baseball mates for a bit of pub crawling.

One evening while Grandma Doris and I were watching a variety show on television, I first saw the Beatles from Liverpool singing *"From Me to You."* I had no idea at the time how big they would become. So many years later, the image of my stately white-haired grandmother Doris comes to mind whenever I hear the Beatle song *"Eleanor Rigby,"* and I find myself wishing her last years were not weighted with loneliness, What did I know of old age back then? I knew Doris was acquainted with a few neighbors and kept involved with her nurses' association, but there were no other children besides my mom, who had gone off to a world away after the war. Could I have known that my presence in her small row house was like her winning a prize vacation, and that my presence filled a vacancy in her life? In the first few days I was there, she got out photo albums and went through them meticulously, attaching stories along the way when she stopped at photos she especially liked. Pausing at a photo of my mother at age 17, dressed in a short athletic skirt, Grandma told me the story about my mom being the fastest girl at her school and had won medals in competitions. Grandma seemed to be living these events again. Then she brought out a picture of my dad in a rakishly cocked white fedora, hands in his pockets, glowing with an insouciant smile, which made Doris lean back onto the sofa and sigh.

"Your father was always such a dandy and so handsome! Evelyn was still a girl and she worshipped him. She thought he resembled the American actor, Robert Taylor! And he was kind to my old Jack and often took him for a pint or two and a chin wag at the corner pub."

I could tell how the past still held her in its embrace. I think my appearance in her life must have given life to the ghosts she lived with.

"I was one of the first people to visit you when you came into the world at Birmingham Central Hospital. Now look at you! All grown up and so much like your dad."

She wanted me to tell her everything I could about my father and mother. I guessed she wanted my point of view. I didn't imagine my mother's short letters gave her too many details. I told her how dad was still in the tool and die business and often played golf on the weekends, and mom had joined a bowling league with other women her age and had won a few trophies. I told her how Mom and Dad would go out sometimes for a drink or two and some dancing on

Saturday nights. Mom would get tipsy and come home in a giggly mood after drinking Salty Jims, a vodka cocktail. This made Grandma Doris laugh.

"Your mum could never hold liquor."

Doris wanted to know about me. So, I told her about my travels on the continent, my athletics through school, about what subjects I most enjoy, and about a few girlfriends, but also that I was in no hurry to settle down. That she was very attentive when I talked about myself impressed me. Grandma Doris had been head nurse of the cardiac ward when she retired. She was much taller than my petite mother, slim and regal with a proud bearing, a bit like the old Queen Mary I'd seen in photos. It was easy to see that Doris had been a beauty in her day.

At the end of the first week of September, the Dunlop baseball team threw a farewell party for me at the club house which also featured a full bar. The baseball season schedule was near an end anyway, and so my departure was not going to matter very much. In eight games I had only four singles and one lucky double because of my running speed, and seven throw-outs to first base. But Percy had tears in his eyes that night when he said goodbye, a good amount of Watney's Ale perhaps making him extra sentimental.

"Well, my Boy, I know you did your best—maybe not what your old dad could have done in his day, but it's been a pleasure to have you. Tell your dad that ole catcher Perce has never forgotten him and sends him signals from home plate wherever he is."

I had a cab pick me up at Grandma's house to take me to the downtown Birmingham train station where I was catching the train to London and Heathrow Airport to board a Pan American flight to Los Angeles the following day. I was out front of her door waiting for the cab with my bit of luggage, and Grandma Doris and I were saying our goodbyes.

"You're still young enough to mind your good mum and dad. Hold them close always. Give a special hug and a kiss to your mum from me."

There were tears welling in her eyes when she grasped me and held me fast. The cab arrived a moment later and she forced something folded into my hand and kept my fist closed with a firm grip. With her other hand, she stroked my face, a parting gesture, as if she wanted to remember its contour.

"Go on now," she said, composing herself.

When I got seated in the cab, I looked at what Grandma Doris had forced into my hand. It was money. In route to the train station, I opened the tightly folded notes and found a ten-pound note and a fiver, almost the equivalence of one week's wages at Dunlop.

I felt brewing tears of shame and sorrow for I hadn't thought to leave her with a parting gift.

On the Road

It was one of those times when Tony wondered how he'd gotten himself into the situation, trying to get some sleep on a humid summer night in a musty lake cabin he'd trespassed, while mosquitos relentlessly assaulted him. He wondered about his resources and why he couldn't have just stayed where he was on the West Coast with sunshine and no mosquitoes. Why wander through the woods of Maine? Perhaps going on the road was mainly a lack of nothing better to do, Tony reflected. Jack Kerouac's book was an empty bill of goods, he thought. It was hard to get romantic about just wanting some sleep when you felt so tired and uncomfortable. Maybe tomorrow with a swim in the lake he could get refreshed, nap on the beach, and then find some place to eat a good, inexpensive meal.

Legend had it that the name of the giant Lake Mooselookmeguntic in western Maine near the Vermont border came down from a story about a local Native American hunting moose. When he'd gotten a moose in the sights of his gun and pulled the trigger, it didn't fire and just ticked. The lake's name really came from the old Algonquin language meaning *moose feeding place*. Indeed, these huge animals were in the neighborhood which Tony abruptly discovered when one came out of the woods a scant twenty yards in front of him, pausing to turn its huge antlered head toward him and then, unconcerned, crossed into the thick woods on the other side of the road.

It was the mid-seventies and Tony had left California on an extended trip to try out theater in the East and act in some shows that might put him on track toward a stage career. That was the dream, anyway. Philadelphia was first on his agenda and Boston second, both cities where he knew people. He might even make it to Montreal where he had an uncle.

In Philadelphia he visited Linda Becker with whom he'd once been involved five years earlier in California. She was happy for his company for a few days and showed him around Philly. She managed a chic women's clothing boutique downtown and had a modest apartment several blocks away where Tony stayed in her spare bedroom which was also her walk-in closet. Linda had always been a clothes horse, owning racks of clothing that got little wear or none. Her downtown location worked out well because Tony found a couple active community theater companies nearby where he might get some action. It was summer and theaters would be mounting their summer repertories and perhaps he could find a theater that was holding open auditions. He hoped his West Coast resume would open some doors. His theater activity in Burlingame, California over the past two years hadn't been extensive, but it was solid with several leading roles in well-known plays. He knew how to read at auditions, and he knew what parts fit and what didn't.

Tony figured if he hooked up with a theater and a show with a run, he'd then find some part-time day work and a place to live. He had lots of experience from greasy spoon breakfast cafes to upscale dinner houses. Those serving experiences coincided with his theater ambitions through three years of continual rehearsals and performances. South Philly, he discovered, was rough but a good place to find cheap studio apartments in old, chopped-up rambling houses. After all, there was no way he could or would stay on with Linda. Their day was long gone.

After four days, Linda was showing signs of impatience. Tony was sure it was his lack of interest in getting intimate with her. He'd thought when they had come to an end in California five years ago and she'd returned to Philly, the flame was extinguished. Linda had always been passionate and needy, but there was no one in her life at the moment. Tony recognized that if he insisted on hanging around, he'd have to perform, but that wasn't in him. He was never so sexual that he could perform without feeling a strong attraction, which was past tense with Linda. On the fourth day of his bunking in, she broached the issue obliquely by asking him where he was headed from Philadelphia. Clear enough. In any case, Tony's visits to the two local theaters had caught them gearing up for productions and his attendance was mostly ignored. His resume was filed by the artistic director at one theater and disregarded by another where plays were already cast until the fall. Tony had forgotten to consider the usual nature of community theaters. They were tight and familial, and strangers appearing on the scene were not readily taken into the company, significant resume or not. His willingness to do almost anything except clean the restrooms had been his way into the Burlingame Contemporary Theater community, but it had still taken time. As the truth sunk in, he decided to scratch the idea of building a theater life in the East and just keep moving, come what may. So, he bid goodbye to Linda with a small bouquet of roses and set out for Boston. He thumbed three rides headed for Boston and found his way to Oliver Fielding's place, an old semi-detached brownstone on Corey Hill.

Oliver was delighted to find him at the door. Tony and Oliver had begun their friendship at the Burlingame community theater where Oliver had been artistic director and later became Tony's mentor. Oly was a tall, elegant gentleman who Tony always imagined playing Caesar or Lear. He was a brilliant director, fifteen years Tony's senior, and had brought Tony along in several major roles, including his co-starring role as Brian in the Pulitzer Prize winning play *Shadow Box*. Oly had come East to fulfill a doctorate in psychology. His partner, Dante Rodriguez, had taught art history at San Francisco State and was now working at Boston College. They were both wonderful cooks and had been Tony's inspiration to develop some expertise in the kitchen.

"You can bunk here in the den. We have guests all the time. Dante will be glad to see you." Oliver smiled and handed him a stack of bedding, towels, and wash clothes. The bath is just around the corner off the hall."

"Don't worry, I won't be staying long. But I couldn't come this way without seeing you and Dante."

Tony filled in Oliver on all that had happened and how he had packed it in at the Burlingame theater. There had been a change in the management and a new artistic director was appointed with whom he didn't get on.

"I just thought it might be interesting to do some theater here in the East. And I got the wild idea to go on the road, you know, budget like."

"Good luck with the theater ambition. Community

theater people here have Broadway sized egos and think of themselves as Broadway bound."

Oly's plan was to get his doctorate and return to California and get certified for family counseling and then set up shop. Dante had spearheaded their move to Boston with his teaching appointment at Boston College.

"When Dante gets home, I'll cook some dinner. I was planning to make *Bouchee a la Reine* and uncork a bottle of Sauvignon Blanc."

"*Booshey* what?" Tony queried. He remembered how Oly was big on French cooking and Julia Child.

"Puff pastry with a lovely vegetable and meat filling. You'll love it."

The first three days with his old friends were a delight. They took him to a community theater to see *When Are You Comin' Back, Red Ryder?*, a tour of the Revolutionary American warship, the USS Constitution, the Waterfront Market, and the Boston Museum of Art. Each night was a new culinary surprise with Dante adding to the mix some of his Spanish dishes, a *Paella Valenciana* and a *Zarzuela de Pescado*.

On Tony's fourth night it was cool and rainy and Oly lit a small fire in the den fireplace. Dante was away at a faculty function. Tony and Oly opened a bottle of Bordeaux and talked. Oliver and Dante had decided they weren't fond of the Boston winters. They were Californians after all. Oly thought he might get back into directing community theater if he had time in his work as a family counselor, but of course that would depend on what theater existed where they resettled in California. He reminded Tony how theater life was fickle. Oliver was interested in what Tony had been planning to do. He praised Tony's stage presence, but it was unlikely that he, like most actors and directors, would ever make a living at it. Most settled for doing community theater for love, not for a living. It was clear now to Tony after his Philly experiences that the idea of finding a way into Eastern US theater was a pipe dream that had grown out of proportion with his successes in Burlingame. Then Oliver brought out a fat joint of pot which they proceeded to smoke, followed by laughter as they recalled some of the problematic, funny actors they'd experienced when they had worked together on Burlingame productions.

"You are truly a beautiful man, Tony."

"Oh, thank you, Oly. You are too."

Oly then put his hand on Tony's shoulder and didn't remove it, his eye contact searching for a response. Tony gave Oliver's hand a gimlet eye and a negative shake of his head, an unequivocal *no*. No words were necessary.

"I'm feeling pretty tired and messed up from the weed, Oly. I'd like to turn in," Tony announced and stood up.

"Thanks for a nice evening, amigo," Oly said, also standing up, and smiling as best he could. Tony wasn't offended, just sorry and embarrassed for Oly and disappointed by Oliver's intended unfaithfulness to Dante. Tony hoped this had been just a one-off situation, although he wondered. He also felt a little flattered that Oly was so attracted to him. But making love with a man was inconceivable for Tony, no matter how much affection he felt for Oliver.

On the fifth day, refreshed from four nights in a comfortable bed and prepared for continuing the journey with a backpack full of cleaned clothes, Tony said his goodbyes to Oliver and Dante and hit Highway 1 NE for legendary Salem, Massachusetts.

He wandered through old Salem, his mind full of

images from Arthur Miller's play *The Crucible*. It was a play he would have liked to direct, recreating the madness and the terror respectively of the accusers and those accused of witchcraft, one of the darkest moments in early America's history. Then he got a ride up to Gloucester and the downtown harbor area where he had a plate of deep-fried local Cod with chips. People were friendlier than on the West Coast or perhaps it was just his luck getting rides. Next, he arrived in Ipswich with some of the most historic old homes in America.

By the time he got to Portland, Maine up the coast, Tony was dead tired and took a room at a cheap hotel, spending some of what precious little money he had left. The next day he felt fit enough to head east across Maine toward Vermont. It was a hot summer but there were lots of lakes as he crossed the state. He stopped several times, found beaches, and took long, refreshing dips and caught naps in the shade. Most public lake fronts had rafts near the shore for swimming and sunbathing, but huge devilish horseflies were everywhere, and they could draw blood with their painful bites if one was unguarded.

The Maine forest and lakes were a paradise, but there were drawbacks with the daunting flies during the daytime and the relentless mosquitoes at night. At Lake Mooselookmeguntic Tony desperately broke into a vacant cabin to escape the mosquitos. He finally got some sleep on a couch, but his scalp was a mass of bumps the next morning from bites sustained during the night. Finding a stretch of beach at the lake, he decided to spend several hours swimming and resting, and as luck would have it, he was able to buy some mosquito netting at a lake bait shop and country store.

On the road again, Tony was thumbing west toward

Vermont, when a long-haired man in his thirties in a beat-up Volkswagen van stopped and introduced himself.

"You look like you could do with a good meal and some rest, brother."

Clive, as he called himself, was headed only a few miles west to his homestead, and he offered Tony a meal at his house. Tony introduced himself.

"My old lady will be whipping up some lunch about now. We don't get too many visitors out here, as you might imagine, so it would be nice to have a visitor from San Francisco. I've always wanted to see the Golden Gate bridge."

Clive was originally from Boston but had moved out into the woods with his wife when they had decided city life was just too complex, hectic, and expensive, and no place to raise kids. Together they had built their house in a clearing in the woods a quarter mile off the highway and had a well drilled. Clive's wife, Chrissy, blonde-haired with a scrubbed, rosy Scandinavian face, welcomed Tony as he entered the house and was introduced by Clive.

"Here you go, Tony, a fresh brewed cup of coffee. Brunch coming up in a jiff," she said. She was slender but muscular, a classic farm-girl type. She and Clive lived off the grid, their power coming from a dozen solar panels on the roof and a big generator for backup.

"Clive, did you get everything on my list?" Chrissy inquired.

"Got it all, Sweetie." Clive had been sent to get supplies thirty miles away at the country store where Tony had bought his mosquito netting. Clive seemed to have a fixed smile, as if every minute of existence was a joy.

Then the room erupted with the sudden entrance of

two little boys from the back of the house. Introduced as Pablo and Django, 5 and 6, who approached Tony and offered their hands, like perfect little gentlemen and told him their ages.

"Pleased to meet you, sir," said Pablo, the oldest of the two.

Minutes later, all were seated, Tony, the boys, Clive, and Chrissy who had served up a huge frittata in an iron skillet, chock full of veggies and beans. When the meal and everyone's life story was finished, Tony was ready to get back on the road. Clive drove him to the best road headed for Vermont, saying he'd look Tony up one day in California. Tony had given Clive his parents' Bay address and phone number. They wouldn't be changing their address and would always know where Tony could be found.

After a long bumpy ride Tony had hitched in an empty horse trailer, he was dead tired and knew he needed a break from the road. He wasn't far now from Montreal. His Uncle Eric had always felt more like an older brother, and Tony knew Eric would be glad to see him.

It was an easy two-hour ride north along Lake Champlain on the Greyhound bus, offering splendid views of the lake, farms, forest, and islands. At the Canadian border, he got out his plastic-wrapped passport, wallet and address book and identified himself to the immigration officer who came aboard the bus. When all passengers had been checked, the bus got on its way again to the great French-speaking city on the St. Lawrence River, where Tony telephoned his Uncle Eric.

Eric, Tony's youngest uncle of four, had a huge, ostentatious red brick mansion in the ritzy Westmount neighborhood of Montreal, Eric had been successful in the dry-cleaning business, having built a small empire of outlets and plants throughout Quebec, Ontario, and the Maritime Provinces. Eric was fifty-four and he'd visited Tony out in California numerous times over the years. He was a gentle, kind man who hit a pro-like drive off the tee. He had two rowdy sons in their early teens and an athletic pretty daughter of 17 who looked up to Tony as if he were her uncle. Eric's wife Aunt Darlene was as agreeable as sunshine, which no doubt helped family cohesion through Montreal's long harsh winters and endless days indoors. Eric was more exhausted than grumpy from work, and he just wanted a satisfying meal and a cigar when he came home from the office at the end of his day, which was usually about 8 pm. He arrived home some evenings so tired, his eyes didn't seem to focus. It was still summer, but Tony hadn't seen Eric going out to the golf course, although he was a great golfer and a member of the Montreal Country Club. It appeared he had little time for recreation.

Tony was given the converted garage apartment next to the pool back of the grand house. It was a great relief after being on the road, and the pool provided a luxurious continuation of the refreshing dips he'd enjoyed in the lakes along the way. Tony was grateful for the respite, but he wasn't a freeloader; so when Eric mentioned needing to get the grounds fixed up, Tony happily volunteered. There was plenty to do on the two-acre estate—mowing, trimming, pruning, reseeding, planting, fertilizing, and weeding. Always a shrewd businessman, Eric held with *quid pro quo* as fundamental.

Eric's boys often joined Tony at the pool during the heat of the afternoons after he had done his yard work during the cool mornings. Layla, the daughter, would sometimes come out and join Tony when the boys weren't around, and she wanted Tony to tell her about life in California, asking endless questions as if she were planning to emigrate. When Tony asked her with a sly grin if she was planning to run off to the sunshine state, she insisted she was just very curious. She wanted to know about Los Angeles—and, of course, Hollywood. Had he ever met any famous actors? He'd exchanged a few words with Michael Douglas, old John Carradine, and Ralph Meeker to name a few; the latter two were old-timers she wouldn't have known. He'd also met a lot of wannabe actors like himself when he was living in West Los Angeles.

"Why are you so fascinated with California?" Tony asked, immediately reflecting he needn't have asked. Starry eyed teeny boppers everywhere dreamed of California and David Cassidy.

"Montreal is really boring," she said, pouting. "I wish I could go out to California and go to college," she said, brightening.

"Have you asked your dad about that?" He knew Eric could afford to send his kids to almost any school they chose, if they qualified academically.

"He'd like me to go to Princeton. Not so far from Montreal, you know."

"You have the grades to get into Princeton?"

"Almost straight As except for Cs in algebra and French."

"The algebra is forgivable, I suppose, but French when you've lived in Montreal your whole life?"

"I didn't go to French schools," she said with an air of pride. Tony had already checked out the neighborhood and noted the high concentration of Anglos. He didn't catch much French at the local market. Eric had grown up poor in a working-class part of Montreal and had gone to French speaking schools, but Tony seldom heard him speak French. It was clear that Montreal was linguistically segregated. Tony's wife Darlene didn't speak any French at all despite having lived her whole life in Montreal.

"I'd love to go to UCLA," Layla said almost in a whisper as if it were a closely guarded secret."

"Why UCLA?"

"They have a great film school." Layla knew more than she had let on.

"I know. That's where Francis "Godfather" Coppola went to school," Tony added.

"Why didn't you stay in California and follow your dream of acting?"

"Because that's all it was—a dream."

Grandma

Rent had gone through the roof to $1200 for Edie's small one-bedroom apartment in a large housing development in north Santa Barbara. It was getting harder for her and just about everyone she knew. Inflation was overwhelming her weekly budget. She'd taken the odd job as a courier, but it cost more to work when you had to pay for your own gas as an independent contractor. The economy was squeezing her from both ends. She knew she wasn't alone, but that didn't make her feel any better. She hoped the coming Social Security increase would take off some of the pressure.

Edie had an aging Dodge pushing 180,000 miles which couldn't last much longer. Getting another car would simply mean going into a lot more debt. Life felt like a series of economic gut punches. Thank God, her health had held up, but she wondered how much longer that would be. After all, she was already 75. She had friends her age who were barely able to walk and others who had emphysema or something else debilitating and they got exhausted walking half a block. She felt lucky, but how long could her health hold out? She'd taken a part-time hostess job at Santa Barbara's Holden's Steak and Seafood which was patronized mostly by an older crowd. Because she'd had prior experience hosting and the manager liked her and thought his patrons would like her, she was hired for two nights a week which helped her pay the increase in rent.

This would be her last trip up to Fresno for a while to see her daughter Brigitte and the grandchildren. Round trips to Fresno cost too much in gas these days to make them with any regularity. Her daughter Brigitte wanted to help but she and her husband Jake didn't have much extra. And Edie didn't like asking for help, not yet anyway. Brigitte and her husband had a lot on their plate and were squeezed like everyone else. When Edie became too old to take care of herself, Brigitte and Jake would put her in the unused guest quarters of their rambling ranch home. Meanwhile, as much as she loved Brigitte and her kids, she loved her independence and living where there was work and where she could be close to the beach which she loved. She had been a beachcomber her whole life. A long walk on the beach could always lift her spirits.

Edie checked in with her courier agency to see if there was anything she could run up to Fresno. She might as well get paid for the trip if she were going that way. They gave her a dozen packages for delivery to Fresno and the nearby Woodland Park area, the suburb where Brigitte lived. With the Dodge gassed up and her collection of oldy-but-goody CDs handy, a thermos of coffee, and a couple of Clif bars, Edie was on her way.

She'd always loved the sense of freedom on the open road. Better than being trapped in an office with someone always watching. She'd keep it at 65 mph and spend a lot of the trip in the right lane. Once she hit the rhythm of the road, she'd shift her mind into pleasantly wandering through her memories while playing CDs from the 60s to the 80s. But she was always alert for speeders and road-rage maniacs. She let them have the road and held onto her dreams. Even when she was young, she had gotten around Los Angeles for ten years without a ticket or an incident. She remembered her tiffs with first husband Randy and how she'd react by jumping in the car and peeling out of the driveway. They had been so in love and so young. She could have stayed with him. She had always prided herself on her resolve and determination. How many women her age could still drive all over the state the way she did? Randy had loved her like a poet, but he had the unreliability of a poet too. Edie didn't believe he wandered while they were together. But she couldn't keep him. She understood that better with time. Young men were restless, especially wannabe poets.

What if? That question always made her flow of thoughts become dreamy and then the facts of the past drifted toward fantasy, and she'd have to catch herself. Make-believe was Randy's world! Now decades later, she still heard from him now and then in brief emails. She had visited him a couple times up north and met his wife of thirty-five years. He'd finally settled down, but he still hadn't written the great American novel he used to talk about. Maybe next year she'd drop in to see them if she got up as far as Sacramento.

Randy used to be so handsome. Fifty years had shot by so quickly and taken all his looks, and hers. We'll, no, she still looked pretty good. She just had to spend a little more time with makeup in the mornings. White haired and wrinkled, Randy looked his age but apparently still danced ballroom, and his sense of humor was still intact.

Edie put one of her oldie-but-goody collections into the CD player that started off with *MacArthur Park* by Richard Harris. Edie remembered the 1968 hit as if it were just yesterday and she smiled, although she wasn't smiling back then. Sweet Randy was on his way out the door. The cake she'd baked and iced never made it to the table. They were done, and he went off to San Francisco to read poetry and get stoned with all the hippies.

She'd arrived at Paso Robles where the traffic was moderate and headed east toward Junction 46 north. *I Just Gotta Get a Message to You* by the Bee Gees had come on when Edie was still recounting the end of the 60s and early 70s. She had loved West LA, those few years after Randy, when she felt as though she'd become a woman of fashion and means, her dyed-blonde hair cut a la Sassoon, and she was still wearing mini-skirts to show off her shapely legs. There had been a host of eligible bachelors, a few affairs, but nothing serious. It was the times. The 70s got crazier. How she loved her '72 cherry red Ford Torino hardtop she'd bought on credit. She loved to cruise Wilshire Boulevard and savor the looks she got and sometimes a whistle. She was making good money in those days, managing a Cal Worthington automotive sales and service office in West LA. Coordinating the office and keeping everything in order had always been one of her fortes and it served her well through several office positions.

In the Torino days, Edie was often told she resembled Joey Heatherton, a popular dancing and singing personality appearing on TV variety shows. She'd even had a few guys approach her with that mistaken identity line. It was hard not to enjoy the attention. Now Herb Alpert's *This Guy's in Love with You* was playing. Her thoughts shifted to Dominic. He was impossibly handsome like Alpert, a proverbial dark, handsome stranger who breezed into her life as smoothly as the ride was now as she picked up Highway 46.

The road was open with few trucks to slow the flow in the right lane. She'd hold her speed and eat a Clif bar. Brigitte had said they could have a little lunch together with the kids when she arrived. She looked in her rear-view mirror, saw no one on her tail, and she thought about Domonic who came into focus. Dominic was Italian on both sides of his family and passionate like the rumors surrounding Latin men. Dominic had romanced Edie as if he'd just stepped out of a movie. But she had also thought Randy was perfect when they met as kids working retail at Bullock's Department store. Back then Edie still had her huge stacks of 45 records that kept her company in her room when she was growing up and dreaming of romance. She'd left them behind when she married Randy. We really don't know anything until we live it, Edie thought. She decided to stop at a rest stop and have a coffee from the thermos.

Fifteen minutes later, Edie was back on the road, remembering Dominic as the 1982 Air Supply hit *Even the Nights Were Better* was playing. Edie and the suave Dominic were married and had baby Brigitte. Her daughter was indeed a dream come true. But not long after Brigitte came into the world, Edie's sweet doting mother passed on with a fatal heart attack. That event was a bigger hurt than divorcing Randy. Edie sometimes dreamed about her mother trying to talk sense to her like she did when Edie was growing up. Her mother left her a substantial legacy which Dominic insisted on managing after they were married. After all, he was the businessman, not Edie. Even so, Edie never thought Dominic's purchasing a racehorse was a good investment, but women of her generation still believed it wifely to defer to their husbands. Dominic convinced her they'd make lots of money from the racehorse as a stud.

She now found herself closing in on a slow semi ahead with a big load of lumber and she had to pass it, which she did and came back down to her cruising speed in the right lane. A new disc played *Do you Know the Way to San Jose?* by Dionne Warwick. Edie knew her way almost everywhere up and down the Californian coast. But then as now, men were still strange, an incomprehensible lot who you could never quite know because they were fickle and slow to grow up.

There had been so much love in the early years of the marriage to Dom, and baby Brigitte grew into a pretty child who Edie loved to dress in all the latest child fashions she could find. Dominic purchased a sailboat that he insisted would make for wonderful family times. Edie, not a good swimmer, never got over being nervous about being on the boat whose sides perilously dipped to the water line. They had also purchased a small ranch home near Santa Paula and bought several mares and a pony for a growing Brigitte who came to love horses. Dominic was chagrined with Edie because, as with the sailboat, she never felt secure on a horse. Brigitte was the opposite, never happier than when she got to ride and care for a horse.

As the 80s progressed, Dominic became more moody, listless, and unapproachable. The 80s recession had put the brakes on the real estate business in which he was employed, and a cloud descended on their house with his moods. Edie managed to get a look at a few bank statements and then realized one reason for his agitation. Their bank accounts and market investment account had shrunk in half. That's when the stallion stud broke a leg and had to be put down, and Dom's black mood deepened. The more Edie pushed for answers, or just rational adult talk, the more aggressive his responses became. Edie learned that Latin passion could also have a flip side. Meanwhile, young Brigitte became frightened by the discord in the house and retreated to her room. One night when Dom was furiously going over papers at the kitchen table and Edie demanded to know about their cratering accounts, he blindly lashed out and caught Edie across the face. Whether he intended to hit her or not, that night while Dom slept, Edie packed enough for herself and Brigitte and fled the ranch and never looked back.

Nine to Five with Dolly Parton was on the next disc. Music did coincide with our lives sometimes! Edie remembered the difficulties she'd had rejoining the work force to support herself and her daughter. It was after the recession in the mid-80s that companies and small offices were hiring again, even in Santa Barbara, where Edie had moved to set up a new life for herself and Brigitte.

She passed Kettleman City and signs for Visalia now appeared, which meant there would be less than an hour to Fresno. She was making good time. Edie's lawyer won her half of what was left of the estate after Dominic's mismanagement and squandering, including sale of the ranch, that came to $170,000. That nest egg lasted just long enough to get Brigitte through high school in Santa Barbara and one year at City College, while Edie worked half time as receptionist at a large dental clinic. Then Brigitte, who had become a gorgeous, slim brunette, went off to LA to seek her fortune as a model. Edie couldn't convince her to stay and finish college. Edie swore to Brigitte that she'd see her through college if she stayed. Edie remembered how she herself hadn't heeded her intuitive mother who advised her against marrying the poetic Randy and then the imposing Dominic.

Funny, how after you get old, Edie thought, hindsight has clear 20/20 vision. The traffic had now thickened as she approached the suburbs of Fresno. She dropped off her deliveries in route through the city to the north and then the balance in The San Joaquin River Estates.

How Brigitte had been pursued in Hollywood, even by a couple of well-known actors, but mostly by a string of second-rate wannabes. Her modeling income was getting as thin as she was at that time when, thank God, she met the reliable, rock-solid Jake who loved horses and was building a lucrative career with John Deere. He was away a lot, traveling to farm areas throughout the state. But he had been good to his word and married Brigitte and bought her a modest country spread and a large house in Rolling Hills and has never laid a mean hand on her.

Barbara Streisand knew how to get you misty with her *Woman in Love* now making Edie reflect on her daughter. Edie knew about Brigitte's Hollywood lovers, but Brigitte had fortunately never conceived. It had been easy for her with Jake, although perhaps a little late at 40, but fortunately her kids were born healthy and beautiful. Edie saw those events as Fate dealing her line some deserved luck. How nice it would be to sleep in Brigitte's quiet country home tonight in those separate quarters reserved for her with a bathroom that featured a deep soaking tub—and a back door to a spacious porch looking out on a grove of Jacaranda trees.

Edie arrived late for lunch, so Brigitte heated up some of her big pot of homemade chicken soup to go with the homemade bread she'd baked especially for Edie. Brigitte looked beautiful, Edie thought, more than when she was trying to make it in the modeling world. She was filled out and softened from the anorexic look she'd had in those Hollywood days. The kids, Stella three and Lorenzo now four, were roughhousing with the family dogs, two young golden retrievers. The dogs became disinterested after a few minutes and the children turned their attention to the mess of plastic Marvel characters spread out on the floor of the living room. Edie could see Brigitte in her granddaughter Stella.

"How's the soup, Mom?"

"You've learned to cook, girl." Edie replied.

"Why don't you stay more than a few days?" Brigitte pleaded.

"Hey, Sweetie, I've got to be back at my restaurant job. But I'll play with the kids while I'm here and give you a break. When are you expecting Jake home?"

"Tonight. He's coming in from Yuba. He's closing a deal on a bunch of farm equipment."

"I don't imagine you get much time to ride these days."

"When Jake's around he'll spell me, so I can get out for a nice long ride. Got a new pretty mare, an anniversary gift from Jake."

Edie surveyed the messy kitchen, the disarray of the adjoining dining area and farther, the living room with toys scattered everywhere. Somehow, she'd never seen her daughter look so beautiful, now without mascara and lipstick, her shiny long hair carelessly stacked in an updo. Edie had once wanted all that she saw, but the men she'd chosen hadn't accommodated. Now she could share it all without the drag and complications. Little Stella and Lorenzo were offering her their treasured Marvel toy characters.

"For you, Gwandma," Lorenzo said, handing her a plastic Captain America.

Edie, in a surge of emotion, pulled both her grandchildren to her bosom and kissed their sweet-smelling heads. She had finally arrived after such a long drive.

Nogales

It was a *capea*, a Spanish custom where the bullring management would let loose a two-year old brave cow into the ring as a preliminary to the main event, and amateurs got to make a few passes, or get tossed which often happened. On rare occasions, a hapless participant would sustain a tossing injury or a horn wound. So, everyone who intended to go into the ring had to sign a disclaimer. For me it was a dream come true to finally get a chance to face an animal. The cows were just as brave as their brothers, usually with less heft, but equally ferocious, and packing horns just as sharp if not as big. In the past year, I had been accumulating knowledge about bullfighting by reading every book I could find, and I spent a lot of time practicing with the cape and the muleta *a la salon*—playing pretend bull and bullfighter with other avid aficionado practitioners from the Los Angeles Aficionado Club.

There were four of us from the Los Angeles club who were going to enter the ring along with several others from the Tucson and Phoenix clubs. We were to perform for the crowd's amusement before the main bullfight with four bulls from the Peñuelas ranch, featuring matadors Joselito Torres and Paco Rodriguez.

The events leading up to the trip to Nogales on the Arizona border were the beginning of a three-year journey for me that was to include a year in Spain. I was at UCLA in my sophomore year in 1961, living in the Sigma Nu fraternity house when I got wind of the Nogales bullfight and preliminary *capea*. My Sigma Nu fraternity brother Billy Barnes offered to fly me to Nogales for the weekend event. Billy was a pre-med major in his third year and had a four-seater Cessna that he often flew down to La Jolla where his family lived. Billy and frat brothers Norm Winters and Vern Reed were excited about going to the border for some bar hopping and carousing in addition to seeing me fight. They were offering me the fourth seat, round trip, just over an hour's comfortable flight.

Emilio Vejar of the Los Angeles Taurine Club was planning to drive to Nogales and offered to take three others in his comfy '56 Buick with AC. Those joining him would be asked to chip in for gas. Fighting bulls was one thing, but flying in small airplanes was another, and after thinking it over, I opted for the drive with Emilio. It would take just over eight hours, starting in the morning and stopping midway somewhere for lunch and then arriving in Nogales around dinner time Saturday evening. Anyway, I wanted to be with my bullfight amigos.

We stayed at the Hotel Olivia not far from the bullring where the rooms were cheap but clean. I didn't get much sleep with the excitement of what I was going to attempt the following day, but at twenty, one's resources ran deep. I had hoped to see Billy Barnes and my other two Sigma Nu brothers at the Olivia sometime that day, but they were late showing up, and as I got involved with my cohorts, Vejar, Armendariz, and Al Greenwood, I forgot about Barnes and company. I figured they'd probably show up closer to the opening of the bullring on Sunday afternoon. It was around

9 am on Sunday when my companions and I were having a small breakfast of *juevos rancheros* and tortillas in the Olivia Hotel dining room. Bullfighters were advised to fast at least eight hours before fighting in case of surgery when an empty stomach is recommended. But aside from that, we knew we weren't going to want any food later anyway because our stomachs would be tightening up with the approach of entering the ring, the adrenaline rush, and the inescapable fear. No one wanted to risk throwing up in the ring anyway, so we'd all feast later that evening after the fight.

Just when we were finishing breakfast and having more coffee, in walked Matador Jorge Baez with Walker Ballard in tow. Baez was a popular bullfighter along the border in the 60s for his flamboyant style, his breath-taking valor and his Latin good looks. He was also known for consorting with Hollywood starlets. He'd taken Walker under his wing and mentored and groomed the handsome blond American for the ring. Walker was slated to step into the ring as an alternate to the matadors Torres and Rodriguez. If one of them was injured and unable to continue to fight, Ballard would substitute as *sobresaliente*. I was sure Jorge Baez had arranged the *sobresaliente* job for Walker, and I felt envious that Walker was so lucky to have a great matador as his mentor and guide. Customary for the *sobresaliente*, Walker would also get the chance to make cape passes with the big bulls during the first third of each fight when the picadors did their work to tame the bulls' ferocity. I knew Walker had gained experience in the interior provinces at bull ranches with young cows and had already fought in several novice bullfights with *erales*, two-year-old bulls. I had read he fought well in those *novilladas* in Toros magazine, a border-circulated,

English-language magazine on bullfighting. Walker cut quite a striking figure with his blond, Yankee good looks when dressed in a contrasting, dark-colored suit of lights. It was common knowledge that gaining entrance into the Mexican bullfighting world was especially hard for Americans and other foreigners because the bullfight coterie was covetous of their world. But, Jorge Baez, being a bit of an outlier and perhaps more than a little Americanized, had been willing to go to some lengths to get Walker launched. In any case, I wasn't ready for big bulls like Walker was. I didn't have any experience at all. The *capea* later that afternoon was to be my baptism. I had borrowed from Billy Barnes an old party outfit, a quasi-traditional Mexican cowboy suit with the short waisted jacket and high waisted pants with spangles down the legs.

While we were in the Olivia Hotel dining room, Paco Rodriguez also came in and took a far corner table by himself. I couldn't ever remember reading about him in Toros magazine. Vejar told me Rodriguez was an old-time bullfighter way past his prime who Joselito Torres, the mainliner, had probably got onto the card as a favor. The buzz from aficionados we met that day was that Rodriguez held the dubious distinction for the most horn wounds of any active Mexican bullfighter. He was a big man, compared to most bullfighters, but he was trim and had a mournful mestizo face scarred by acne.

A bit before 4 pm, we all lined up in the tunnel entrance into the ring and when the trumpet blew and the big gates were swung open, we marched into the almost full ring of several thousand fans and across to the opposite side, saluted the judge above, and took our places behind the barrera, the fence lining the interior sand. I had to use all my will to calm my heart. The trumpet sounded again for the toril gate to be opened and a moment later our brave cow exploded into the ring in a rage, head and horns held high in challenge, and circled the ring, looking for a target. I thought the cow was bigger and had more menacing horns than any of us had expected and no one was rushing to take the challenge. The cow stood proudly near the barrier and snorted, its head and horns held high.

Then Vejar stepped out and called to the beast, and it charged in an instant, tossing him over the barrier like a rag doll, eliciting a collective moan of dismay from the crowd. Then Raul Armendariz came out on the sand, but as the cow sped at him, he turned and vaulted over the fence, the cow's horns barely missing his rear end. Greenwood stood pale and frozen behind the barrier and never attempted to step into the ring and engage the animal. Meanwhile I had come out onto the sand to the middle of ring away from the barrier where the cow seemed to be its most dangerous, and I called out to the cow, citing with a shake of my cape.

I was in my dream come true, floating the cape out for the cow in four perfectly, flowing *Veronica* passes in succession, as I had done in a hundred practice sessions, keeping the silk just ahead of the sharp tips of the horns. Then I made a finishing sweep, bunching the cape to my side in a half *Veronica* so that the cow turned in so sharply in its attempt to gore the cape that it was momentarily bewildered and paused to reorient. The *oles* and subsequent applause for my series of *Veronica* passes made me forget about my adversary and I started to walk away with my head turned up to the crowd's adoration. The next thing I knew I was flying into the air and came down hard on the sand, the wind knocked from me. I had forgotten the principal rule of the ring that you never take your eyes off the bull! Fortunately, one of the ring masters quickly lured the cow away when I was prone on the ground and a perfect target for a goring as the cow zeroed in on me with lowered horns. After another fifteen minutes of being played by the other *capea* participants, the flagging cow was led out of the ring and back to the corrals beneath the ring by one of the capea assistants. The ring was then cleared and prepared for the beginning of the main event, the *corrida* with Torres and Rodriguez. All of us *practicos* were instructed to stay behind the barrier and not create any distraction to the bulls and keep the passageway behind the barrier open. The *Cielo Andaluz*, the traditional entry pasodoble began with the brass, and the *cuadrilla* gates swung open and out stepped Torres and Rodriguez with their retinues lined up behind them. Walker, the *sobresaliente*, stood between the two matadors to make the entry across the sand. We amateurs had appetized the spectators, and now they were primed to watch the professionals. The Peñuelas bulls were magnificent, all over 400 kilos, well-armed, and itching to fight.

The first two bulls were *manso*, meaning cowardly and indecisive with erratic, choppy charges that didn't permit the toreros to produce any art. With the third bull of the afternoon, Torres did everything, including cape passes I'd never seen before, and he placed his own *banderillas*, the colorful barbed sticks, with balletic grace. Contrary to the first two bulls, the third attacked with ceaseless committed charges bent on goring the lure of the cape and muleta. Torres was the measure of the bull and gave everything he had and was awarded ears and ovations for his bravery and art as he circled around the ring to applause.

Old Paco Rodriguez rose to the challenge of the fourth and last bull of the afternoon, showing the crowd a display of classical bullfighting with *Veronicas* that recalled photos I'd seen of the great gypsy master Gitanillo de Triana. After the *picadores* and *bandilleros* had done their work, Paco solemnly walked to the center of the ring, raised his *montera* hat to the crowd, and turned a 180 in dedicating to the hushed spectators. He threw his *montera* over his shoulder, and he spread out the muleta, the small red cloth, with his sword and stood calmly, loudly calling the bull to battle, "Ehey, Ehey! Toro!" The noble Peñuelas bull, hearing and seeing Rodriguez in the center of the ring, broke into a murderous sprint. In the split second before the bull was about to take the cloth lure, Paco swung it behind his back and the bull instantly changed trajectory and passed behind the old torero by inches, a perfectly executed pendulum pass. The astonished crowd then belonged to Paco, and he proceeded with long, slow right-handed passes, leading the horns low around his legs. After two series with the right hand, he went to the left hand and did the same. Then he did a series of *Manoletinas*, high body passes, while appearing to look away up into the stands, which the crowd loved. Just when the crowd was peaking with delirious response, Paco lined up his bull and killed it with a classical *volopie*, flying feet, going over the horns and down with the sword to the hilt between the bull's withers, a completely honest and life risking thrust, a moment of unquestionable truth when both adversaries' lives hung in the balance. The crowd went crazy and became a sea of waving white handkerchiefs demanding the ultimate recognition from the judge, who accorded by awarding Paco two ears and the tail. The old torero had won the day.

It was indeed a memorable day for bullfighting, including my baptism into the ritual, engaging an animal for the first time. Walker Ballard also had a good day, giving brave elegant *Gaonera* and *Chicuelina* passes to all four bulls, sweeping them by with only inches to spare between the sharp horns and his torso. Flushed with my small glory that afternoon, I no longer felt envious of Walker but only admiration, believing that one day I would triumph equally well, caping the big bulls as he had.

That evening at the hotel, our caravan got drunk in the bar, me included. Al Greenwood didn't appear and retired early. Raul had run from the cow, but at least he had entered the ring and confronted the cow. Vejar, who had been tossed in his encounter, wore his bruises like badges of courage. Dick Fallon, a well-known photographer from Tucson, congratulated me on my performance and got my address at the Sigma Nu house in Westwood, promising he'd send some photos of my veronica passes once he had developed and printed them.

It was a long nine-hour ride back to Los Angeles, all of us with hangovers, except for Greenwood who drove. But my elation over having confronted a live animal and having performed well took the edge off my pain. We stopped briefly in Tucson and had a brunch of Menudo soup and tortillas which eased our hangovers.

After being dropped off in Westwood Monday evening, I slipped into the Sigma Nu house through the back door, went up to my room on the second floor and crashed for twelve hours. On Tuesday morning, when I came down to the dining hall, ravenously hungry, I was approached by our fraternity president Blaine King at breakfast.

"We've been looking for you, Man. We knocked your door."

"Sorry, I was exhausted and slept like the dead. What's up?"

"I guess you wouldn't know, Barnes didn't make it to your bullfight down in Nogales."

"Oh shit, I forgot about those guys. I got so caught up in everything. So, they didn't make it after all?"

"Not only that, Barnes crashed the plane in the San Gabriel mountains. They never made it far from the city."

I had no words in my half-awake state. The awful power of a metal structure crunching and compressing around one's captive body reeled through me as I recalled the T-bone car collision I'd had out on Burbank Boulevard a year before. Luckily, I was only badly bruised and in shock for several hours.

"So …tell me, for Christ's sake!"

"Reed and Winters are in the hospital with some cuts, bruises and fractures, so they're going to make it all right, but……"

"Barnes?"

King pressed his lips together tightly, shook his head and looked down.

"Oh, shit, no!" I said, my mind flashing blank. Blaine put his hand on my shoulder in a gesture of condolence.

"It's not your fault. It was foggy out there and we were told by the authorities he shouldn't have been flying that route," he said.

He told me about the memorial for Barnes and that most of the fraternity brothers would attend. He also told me the hospital where I could visit Reed and Winters. I felt a residual of my hangover returning with a throb. I swallowed hard with the thought I had almost gone on that plane. It was a weekend and an incident I never related to my parents.

A month after the Nogales *capea* and the plane crash, the celebrated blond American bullfighter Walker Ballard met with a mishap in the Reynosa ring along the Texas-Mexican border. In the early phase of a fight with a fresh bull, Walker had dropped to his knees to pass a fast-charge with a showy *farol de rodillas*, a sweeping flourish of the cape that changes the animal's trajectory, only Walker's timing had been off just enough that the bull ran right over him. He wasn't gored, but badly mauled and trampled before his ring assistants could lure the bull away. I heard through the Los Angeles Aficionado club that he was left with a permanent limp and a bad right shoulder that forced him to retire from the ring. A year later, Walker's charismatic, flamboyant mentor Jorge Baez died in a car collision on a highway near the city of Morelia, Mexico.

Two Gentlemen of Sedona

Rex and Liam had easily become friends, both almost eighty, codgers. They knew what they were and who they were. They had retired to Sedona in the late 90s after long careers, Liam as an engineer with Douglas Aircraft in Los Angeles and Rex as a police officer in the Bay area. In the intervening retired years in Sedona, they both lost their wives of many years to illness. So, when the widowers crossed paths on a Sedona senior five-kilometer run, it was easy for them to bond because they ran together at the same slow speed all the way to the finish line. They were in relatively good shape but otherwise partially lost like most old men in their circumstance. Slow jogging and walking the high desert trails of Sedona in the fresh, sweet-smelling mornings gave them an addictive, settling sense of existential wonder. They didn't have grown children with kids or other relatives tempting them away to relocate, and so they were in Sedona for the duration.

They delighted in their Wednesday breakfasts at Wildflower Bread Company, and the view of the majestic red rock mesa from the restaurant deck, a ritual they had now enjoyed for two years. They knew a lot about each other, but things were kept fresh by their review of current events each week, what the past week had brought and how their minor ailments were or weren't improving. Like most retired men their age, they felt the world was coming to no good and they were dumbfounded by the incompetence of their city council on up to the United States Congress. They agreed that smart phones were an encumbrance and made the younger set intrinsically more stupid by their constant reliance on the hand-held device. Although they often said they wouldn't want to be young again, they secretly wished they could be. No one enjoyed the dimming of the light. And being men, however old, they still fantasized about young pretty women.

"Rex, did you ever get around to watching that recent Academy pick for best movie?"

"Pure crap. The Academy does nothing to teach public taste, they only echo the public's lack of it. *Everything, Everywhere, All at Once.* What a gimmick."

"Interesting isn't it, everything is a scam or other these days. The media talk endlessly about inflation, but do they mention in the same breath that corporate America and the stock market are doing fine?"

"Somebody's making money hand over fist."

It was only eight o'clock in the morning and the sunlight on the red rock mesa was beginning to flame up, a scenario that never failed to lighten the spirits of the men and remind them of their privileged existence both in age and place. But that didn't stop them from complaining.

"Now we got a Fed-budget wrangle going on. The Republicans are saying we're spending too much but they have amnesia about Trump's trillion-dollar tax cut to the rich," Liam said as he stared at the glowing Mesa.

"I still haven't forgotten about Bush's tax cuts to the rich."

"Everything is geared to distribute the wealth upwards."

"And the GOP is trying to block money to modernize the IRS."

"The Democrats say the IRS can't do its job," added Rex.

"Losing billions in taxes! The fat-cats don't pay their fair share."

"Why would a working Joe vote for the GOP?"

"Not an ounce of critical thinking in the MAGA mob."

"Hey, what greatness are the MAGAS talking about anyway?"

"I've never been able to figure it out."

"Maybe, make America white again?"

"Make it uniform again?"

"Make it passive again?"

"Make it ignorant again."

"Hey, we're on a roll here."

"I guess they're thinking about the fifties."

"All we cared about was rock and roll then."

"And pussy."

"Check the language, Here it comes to our table!"

"Good morning, gentlemen!" It was a new waitress, a gorgeous new girl, college age, built like a rare mature beauty with a Gina Lollobrigida figure and a sweet smile ear to ear displaying perfect teeth.

"My name's Bodhi and I'll be serving you," she said and handed them menus.

"That's quite an unusual name," Rex commented.

"My parents were into Buddhism—Bodhi is short for Bodhisattva, someone who has attained the highest level of enlightenment."

"Well, have you, Darling'?"

"Perhaps someday. I'll be back to take your order," she said with the same beautiful smile, turned and left. The men looked at each other drawing deep breaths. Neither wanted to show how disturbing her appearance was. They just tacked to another topic.

"The kids these days are all in smart phone Nirvana," Liam said, looking toward a young couple at a nearby table with their heads stuck in their phones.

"So many smart phones and still so much stupidity," Rex added.

Neither Liam nor Rex had smart phones. They saw their lack of the popular personal device as a badge of distinction. But they did have antiquated flip-top phones.

"I told my fifty-year-old son the other day to use his smart phone to analyze himself and ask it if it's normal never to call one's old father. He said he doesn't call because I'm a smart-ass and a know-it-all," Rex complained.

"I don't know if having kids was worth it." Liam avowed.

"Here we are the grousers and groaners society." Rex was always aware of their slide into complaint. It didn't feel right to simply be smiling all the time and celebrating their being above ground. On the other hand, they would pause to acknowledge that one more of their poker acquaintances had passed.

"Did you know Howard Stubbs passed last week?" Rex said.

"No, really? I saw him at the supermarket just a week ago."

He probably wanted his wife to bury him on their ranch property, if that's possible." Rex said.

"How do you know that?"

"I don't, I'm just guessing. He was such a cheap fuck."

"I didn't know him very well."

"He was okay, I guess, just cheap. He could step on a dime and tell you if it was heads or tails." Rex said and continued perusing his menu.

Liam was easy-going, good-natured, and loved everybody and was well-liked. But he shared some common gripes with Rex such as hating Trump.

"When are they going to indict Trump for January six?" he said.

"Don't hold your breath," Rex replied and sipped his coffee. "He's got a cadre of super lawyers greasing his escape."

Waitress Bodhi appeared at their table, reigniting the old men.

"Well, what'll it be, boys?"

The men took an awed look at the pretty young waitress and gave each other a raised eyebrow, a mix of awe and pleasure. After a long pause in which each of them covertly surveyed the curvaceous geography of her body clad in tight-fitted jeans and a short-sleeved blouse that hugged the slopes and valleys of her breasts, they fumbled with their menus. Her calling them *boys* had not been misplaced. They weren't too old to ogle at a wonderfully put-together young woman. Usually, they went for the senior special but now they suddenly changed. They both ordered the Lumber Jack special—steak and eggs, a breakfast for real men.

As the young waitress collected the menus, Rex and Liam had to make an effort to be polite and not over-ogle her.

"Jesus, man, you just about had your tongue hanging out, Rex!"

"You looked like you were petting a bone under the table."

"Don't I wish," Liam retorted.

It was that kind of morning when the appearance of this especially delicious young waitress had flipped their habit of complaining and piqued their softer side they rarely brought to the table.

"She makes me want to recite poetry."

"Too early in the morning for that, Liam."

"You remember how it was always hard in the mornings?"

"Yeah, *that's* a fond old memory."

"No Viagra needed!"

The men went quiet then as if they had gotten lost in their reveries. Liam ran a comb through his sparse hair and Rex looked around at the booths near them.

"How's the old '65 Mustang running, Rex?" Liam asked his friend.

"A lot more fun than your Hyundai?"

"Girls are not impressed by cars anymore, Rex."

"Nevertheless, I enjoy it."

Then waitress Bodhi appeared and topped off their coffee cups.

"Your breakfast is coming up momentarily," she said with a melting smile that fired the men up with anything but thoughts of food. Rex couldn't restrain himself anymore.

"You have a lovely smile, young lady, that brightens everyone you serve."

"Well, thank you."

"Say, could you bring me some A-1 sauce to go with the steak?" Liam asked.

"Of course," she said, pivoted and left, both men following the sashay of her sculpted rear. Liam sighed.

"They say old age is man's biggest surprise, but they don't tell you the nasty surprises keep coming, one after another."

"Liam, I'm surprised how I forget stuff. I write things down on Post-Its, but I still forget stuff. I've had a note for days to get some new razor blades, yet here I am with this four-day scratchy thing on my face."

"I forget to take my meds.," Liam said, shaking his head with resignation.

"How many do you have to take?"

"Too many."

"I'm up to five."

Waitress Bodhi was back again carrying their breakfast plates, a new A-1 bottle tucked under her arm.

"Here you go gentlemen, and here's your A-1. Can I get you anything else?"

The men were trying to stifle lascivious grins in response to her question.

"Could the cook spare the steak?" Rex waved a hand at his plate.

"Don't let it bother you, Miss Bodhi. Don't say a word to the cook. Go take care of your other tables."

Liam agreed that the steak was a bit on the skimpy side and looked something like a uniform piece of pressed meat from a package.

"We should have stayed with the senior eggs and bacon special, a better deal," Liam complained after the waitress left.

"We're getting shorted with everything these days. Just about everything has been reduced except the prices. My favorite cereal comes in a smaller box, but the price is the same."

"Inflation, my man."

"I'll say, sixteen bucks for a breakfast with a puny piece of steak!"

"And another three bucks for the coffee!"

"The only consolation is the waitress."

"I guess the management figures they have to soften the rip-off somehow with cute service."

"Hard to complain to a pretty face, and no tattoos for a change."

"And I'll bet they're not paying her more than six or seven bucks an hour?"

The men settled into their breakfast plates and ate quietly without more of their grumpy banter. They had gotten well into their plates when waitress Bodhi appeared again with a coffee decanter. A young woman like Bodhi had the effect of momentarily changing their whole world view and their sense of time as if transporting them back to their youth when they were always eager to elicit a smile from a pretty face.

"I do hope they're paying you a good wage. A lot of people resigned during the Covid epidemic. Hard to keep employees." Rex spoke as if a commentator on PBS.

"Is eight dollars an hour, okay?" Bodhi innocently responded. "I mean, I make out pretty good with tips."

"We have no doubt about that. But I'd say ten bucks an hour at least would be more appropriate."

"Let her be," Liam interjected, "you're making the kid uncomfortable."

"Naah, she's an intelligent young woman, aren't you, Bodhi?" Rex persisted.

Then the old men began feeling fatherly toward the girl because that was what she was, just a girl after all. Their lust had suddenly fizzled away.

"Just what you need, right? A couple old codgers upsetting your morning," Liam said.

"We're old and gnarly and you innocently remind us of how we once were, young and handsome. They should have old Mavis serving the tables with fossils like us." Rex said, nodding at Mavis at a table nearby.

They made a point of not sitting at Mavis's tables because she gave them no pleasure with her crotchety service, complaining about everything as if it were entertaining to her diners.

"You guys are nice, and I didn't mean to get you worked up. You remind me of my dad. Well, he's a bit younger," Bodhi said.

"Whoa, Just what we needed to hear, right, Grandpa Liam?" Rex gave a fake smile across the table to his friend.

"Would you guys like more coffee?"

"No thanks, Hon, we want to walk out of here, not fly," Liam quipped. The young waitress smiled wanly and left.

The men's eyes trailed after her tight-fitted jeans, and they sighed almost in unison.

"There was a time when I'd have had a raging rocket for that sweet piece," Rex said, leering after Bodhi.

"Don't be so crude," Liam chided.

"Truth is crude, and aging makes us truthful," Rex continued.

"I don't want to know," Liam said, giving Rex the face of his changing mood, stirring more sugar into to his coffee.

"Can you remember your last good piece?"

"None of your goddam business, Rex."

"Liam, we don't want to face the facts, we're shells now, like the broken, dried-up things you find washed up on the beach."

"Speak for yourself."

"The waitress reminds us that we have nothing left. Not even Viagra helps, right?"

Liam wasn't responding now. He just looked uncomfortable with Rex's ranting.

"Come on, Liam. Tell me, what are we supposed to do now? Hobbies? Go to Mass? Sit with the Buddhists in the south of town? Feed the pigeons at the park?"

"Jesus, you got up on the wrong side of the bed today, Rex!"

"No, I was fine until we got that superb little piece serving us today."

The men became like so many older couples one sees in restaurants, each looking around and lost in thought as if alone at the table.

Waitress Bodhi arrived with the separate tab trays they had requested and left them on the table with a forced smile.

"You know, Rex, you criticize others like you did Stubbs, may he rest in peace, but I've seen how you contribute to the poker gatherings—like bringing dirt-cheap bottles of California Mondavi wine and bags of crappy potatoes chips. What kind of contribution do you call that? And when the evenings are over, you take home your unfinished bottle of rotgut and a half-eaten bag of chips. Talk about cheap. You're pathetic."

"And you, Liam, are always acting superior, above everything and everybody."

"Your parsimony infects everything you do. You have nothing to offer anyone. There's not a generous bone in your body. Rex, the king of cheap."

"And you sail through life unfazed by the injustices and suffering around us everywhere."

"Now, boys, let's calm down. Others are looking at you two. You're creating a scene." It was the battle axe waitress Mavis, hands on her broad hips and a sharp frown on her face.

"Our apologies, Mavis, we'll cool it, won't we, Rex?"

"You two ought to be ashamed of yourselves squabbling like a couple of schoolboys. Pay your tabs and call it a morning!"

The men composed themselves, rechecked their tabs on the little trays and took out their wallets.

"There, an extra five for the young waitress for putting up with you, Rex," Liam said, laying down a five-dollar tip.

"King of cheap, you say, huh?" Rex responded. "There! And fuck you," he blurted, slapping down an extra ten spot on his tray.

Sumo

Their first home in Nagoya, Japan was a ground floor apartment in what reminded Dan of a bleak Eastern European block-residence, eight floors high and eight units across. But at least the units all had small verandas where wash could be hung. Dan learned from a fellow teacher from Michigan that their type of dwelling was often called an *eel home* because it was narrow and only had light at the entrance and at the back-end veranda, a tunnel. Because the living space, apart from the vinyl floored kitchen, was fitted with the traditional grass weaved *tatami* mats, Dan and his wife Penny soon got used to not wearing shoes and padded about in their socks. Still young in their early thirties and from among the working poor back in California, they took to their new foreign home with hopeful relish. The apartment was clean and refurbished, the sliding *shoji* doors fitted with new rice paper panels and the newly installed *tatami* mats were still green and sweet smelling. Their rent, for a change, didn't take the lion's share of their income.

It was liberating to not have a car. A ten-minute walk from the door took them to the Ueda Station on the Tsuramai subway line that took them wherever they needed to go in the city. They were assigned conversational English classes in the evenings somewhere between five to nine and so their days were free. They would often leave a crock pot simmering stew for when they got home around 9 pm, or they'd meet at Ito's sushi shop steps away from Ueda Station.

They had arrived in the fall and so they adopted the Japanese custom of drinking warmed up sake in the cold evenings after work. They also quickly adopted the custom of soaking in the *ofuro,* their sunken Japanese tub, and sleeping on the *tatami* floor with a roll-out futon. The language was a challenge, but fortunately, most Japanese were friendly, accommodating and patient. Dan and Penny even quickly became minor celebrities at Ito's sushi shop where the regulars would buy them drinks and practice their meager knowledge of English. Ito-San was a consummate host at his *sushi-ya* and he gave Dan and Penny special attention, always offering them a complimentary taste of something when they came in. They were not new to sushi. It was the early 80s and sushi was available in California, but some things on Ito's menu were new to them like the urchin roe. Ito would put a bright orange mound of the spiny sea creature's roe on top of a round of sticky rice encircled with a strip of *nori* seaweed. Ito would watch them intently as would some of the bar's cronies for their reaction to the Japanese delicacy, and they were delighted by Dan's and Penny's pleased satisfaction with the taste treats. If the *gaijin* loved their special traditional food, it was a sign by extension the outsiders loved Japan and the patrons of the shop. Dan and Penny became confirmed patrons of this little world of the sushi shop when they showed they could use chop sticks and made concerted efforts to utter a few words in Japanese. Of course, all this international bonhomie was well-oiled with continual rounds of warmed sake with the traditional toast of *kampai* initiating the downing of every jigger. By the time they would leave the shop, the short walk home to their apartment in the winter was sobering and refreshing and made them ready for sleep which came quickly when they cuddled on their Japanese futon.

After work one cold night in December, Dan and Penny went to the *Sushi-ya* to watch some of the Sumo Basho on TV, the seasonal tournament broadcast from Tokyo. It was an especially curious spectacle featuring 300-400-pound men with feudal, top-knot hairdos, tossing and pushing each other around in a ten-foot ring. The favored star was Chiyonofuji who reminded Dan of Bolo Yeung, the famed martial arts movie star. Chiyo wasn't rotund and fat like most sumo wrestlers but a sculpted mass of muscle and he was lightning fast. Smaller than many of the huge sumo grapplers, Chiyo would often win his matches with a speedy maneuver that got his larger opponents off balance and easy to push out of the ring or to the hard sandy floor. Dan and Penny sat at the bar, eating rolls of *makizushi* and sipping sake.

"You like Konoshiki?" Ito asked. Small Japanese bars of every description usually had affable owner-operators who interacted with patrons, but Ito-San was an extrovert where most Japanese were somewhat reserved. Among many of Ito's skills was the art of conversation in a little English.

"*Dare?*" Dan queried. He could produce a few words and phrases, but he found it difficult to understand spoken Japanese.

"Konoshiki America *Ozeki*. Ozeki was a designation for a second-tier champion, just below the grand champion, the *Yokozuna*.

Dan was still new to Sumo and didn't know about Konoshiki.

"American very big, 300 kilo," Ito said, making a wide circular gesture with his arms. "Hawaii man."

"Holy cow!" Penny said, "that's over 600 pounds! I've got to see this guy."

"Big fat like *kujira*," Ito said, as he sliced off slivers of succulent *maguro* sushi from a large chunk of red tuna. Penny had already opened her little Berlitz dictionary.

"Whale! He's big as a whale! Kujira!" she exclaimed.

They anticipated seeing the much-vaunted Hawaiian sumo wrestler while consuming more sushi and drinking sake.

The tournament went on for 15 days with all the wrestlers competing in 15-bout round robin. Dan was able to gather that the one left with the most wins won the tournament. Chiyonofuji, Wakashimazu and Konoshiki were those leading the pack so far with 5 wins apiece.

They stayed long enough to watch the big Hawaiian Konoshiki easily defeat his opponent and then they left the sushi bar around 11:00 pm, a little tight with sake but exhilarated by an evening away from the apartment where they spent so much of their free time. During that winter they spent many cold evenings, sitting on the *tatami* floor with legs tucked under the low *kotatsu* table that had a heating element on the underside. They warmed themselves while reading and sipping hot tea. Penny had already been through three of James Michener's voluminous novels and all of Colette's, and Dan had finished several of John Updike's novels and John Cheever's collected stories. And they played endless games of cards and checkers. Getting out and socializing with the people was a relief and made them feel they were getting the most out of the adventure they had undertaken. Besides, they were beginning to accumulate some handy vocabulary, and some bits of Japanese experience were settled into clarity.

They went to Ito's sushi shop to watch the final bouts from the Tokyo Sumo Basho, and they planned to have their evening meal at the Ito *sushi-ya*. Regulars Kenji-San and Osamu-San were already at the bar drinking *miswari*, Suntory whisky on the rocks with a dash of water. Dan had acquired a sort of language exchange with them, learning new words and phrases as they realized he could understand some short phrases if spoken slowly. It seemed they were amused to have an American in their midst who enjoyed their national sport and ate and drank with them. Indeed, Dan was enjoying his immersion in this Japanese company while Ito's wife Hiromi, who usually remained in the back quarters of the shop, came out and made conversation with Penny. Hiromi was pretty, in her early 40s and like so many educated Japanese women, she had learned some conversational English during her school years. The evening turned into a real party. That night, Ito brought out his daughters Eiko and Aiko, 10 and 11 respectively, who were already learning English in elementary school, and they were delighted to greet and say a few words with Penny and Dan.

Wakashimazu was beaten by Takanosoto so that now only Chiyo and Konishiki, the giant Hawaiian, remained unbeaten with fourteen wins apiece. Chiyo was up against the formidable Kitanoumi and the sushi bar went silent to focus on the TV. The big men held onto each other's *mawashi* waist sash to gain leverage, but neither could move the other, until Kitanoumi got Chiyo off balance enough to cause him to step over the ring boundary for a loss. If Konoshiki won his bout with Musahimaru, he'd win the tournament. The Hawaiian was at his best weight near a quarter ton and his best offense was his thrusting and slapping. Chiyo had already proven Konoshiki's weight could be his weakness and gravity would work against him with the slightest imbalance. Musashimaru looked more like a Mafia soldier than a Japanese wrestler. But Konoshiki's powerful thrusts forced Musashimaru to put a foot out of the ring. The bar exploded with hoots and hollers. Konoshiki's win gave him a perfect record of 15 wins, making him the winner of the winter tournament and the first foreign wrestler to win the sumo title! Dan and Penny were treated to sushi and drinks by Ito and the regulars as if they were part of Konoshiki's victory.

That same night, Kenji-san invited Dan to a party the following weekend, a short cab ride from the neighborhood. The party was going to celebrate local lower-division sumo wrestlers. The party was being given by a Mr. Kiyoda, a wealthy, rabid fan whose house and gardens were magnificent in the old traditional style. It was an all-male affair with lots of food and sake. Dan managed to sort this all out, using his pocket dictionary and Kenji using his. They would meet up at Ueda station. Penny didn't mind. She wasn't interested in going to a party where there were no other women. She also advised him she was off drinking anyway. There had been too much for her with their recent partying at Ito's *sushi-ya*. She wanted to take a break and she also admonished Dan to go easy with the sake.

During that week everything went as usual. They watched the English language TV they got in Nagoya— *MASH* and *Little House on the Prairie* and they read. Penny did their shopping at Hallo Market and the U store. Dan had a few private classes in their apartment with a couple university students and another with a couple of salary men he'd met on the subway coming in from downtown one day.

In both cases, he was paid $50 per hour, a handsome fee for such easy work. Penny did a few private classes, teaching a pair of women at their apartment, and two stations up the line at Yagoto station, she gave a class for several children which mainly consisted of playing games in English.

When Dan went with Kenji-san, Penny left for downtown to shop at Maruei and Mitsukoshi department stores for a warm scarf, something she didn't bring from California and needed with winter temperatures dropping in Nagoya.

The party at the Kiyoda house was held in an expansive room about the size of a tennis court with *tatami* mat flooring. Everyone entering had to leave their shoes at the broad entrance. Mr. Kiyoda was a dignified man nearing eighty and spoke a fair amount of English. He'd been a CEO with Datsun in his day, having spent some time in the US during the Japanese automobile revolution that took hold in California in the mid-sixties with the small reliable Datsun cars. Kiyoda liked Americans and warmly greeted Dan when introduced by Kenji-san.

"So, you enjoy Sumo?" he inquired.

"I enjoy it very much, Kiyoda-san."

"Where are you from in America?" he asked.

"Los Angeles."

"I know Los Angeles very well. Sandy Koufax was great pitcher, I see him many times," Kiyoda exclaimed, smiling with pleasure at recalling the great Los Angeles Dodgers' pitcher.

He told Dan to enjoy the party, to eat and drink a lot and thanked him for coming. There was a cadre of women in everyday kimono shuffling about the huge banquet room in white *tabi* socks, putting *bento* box lunches at place settings along the low-slung Japanese tables. Tall bay windows to the side of the room provided a view of a magnificent Japanese garden full of ornamental evergreens, and a huge Koi pond spanned by a Chinese arched bridge. Dan estimated attendance at near a hundred guests, including a dozen young *sumotori* from the lower *sandanme* division, aspirants to the higher professional levels. About ten minutes after Dan and Kenji arrived, the crowd began to settle down on the *tatami* mats at the tables in the traditional squat manner, and Mr. Kiyodo addressed the room from a microphone. Dan could only guess it was a welcome speech to everyone and some information about sumo, including an introduction of the young *sumotori* wrestlers in attendance. The kimonoed women went about setting warmed carafes of sake on the tables and the men went about pouring off jiggers for each other. Kenji poured off a jigger for Dan and Dan reciprocated pouring for his friend. They voiced the usual *kampai* and took the sake down in single shots. They continued these shooters until the kimonoed women brought them the bento box lunches consisting of deep-fried shrimp in panko, a piece of sauteed red snapper, several pieces of sushi with bite-size slabs of raw tuna along with a small bowl of rice and one with miso soup, a filling lunch much needed with the quantity of sake everyone was consuming, including Dan and Kenji. The women kept on replacing emptied carafes with full ones.

It was three hours later when the festivities started to break up and people were packing it in. Dan had trouble getting up and felt wobbly when he did. Kenji appeared worried about him, but Dan kept saying *Dai jo bu, Dai jo bu*, it's okay, it's okay. Fortunately, there was a line of cabs waiting in the circular drive and Kenji got them back to Ueda and Dan's apartment. Dan passed out during the ride back, and Kenji had to help him to his apartment door when they arrived. He knocked on the door and Penny answered. As Kenji stepped across the threshold, supporting Dan, Dan collapsed. Penny thanked Kenji who went on his way, and Penny helped Dan to the extra bedroom near the apartment front door. It was probably going to be a rough night for Dan, and so she decided it was best for him to be on his own. Penny knew there would have to be an end to the drinking.

Dan was painfully hung over the next day and not in a mood for anything other than soaking in the *ofuro* and drinking cold water for his dehydrated state. By late afternoon, he recovered to where Penny felt she could talk to him.

"While you were at your party, I was downtown in Sakai, shopping at Mitsukoshi, and I went to see Doctor Hatano."

That announcement momentarily shook Dan out of his torpor. Hatano was the doctor in Sakai whom their employer told them to contact if they had a health problem. He was fluent in English and had an American wife.

"Are you all right?" he queried.

"The party's over, Dan."

"What?"

"I'm pregnant."

Eliot and Esther

Eliot Caldwell was a businessman, a sportsman and one of the finest gentlemen I had ever met. I often told him he was too nice to be a Republican. Just because his family had always voted Republican was not a good enough reason to continue, I told him. He'd also been an alcoholic, but he'd finally gotten a handle on that problem and had been on the wagon with the *twelve-step program* for ten years.

I met Eliot at our city athletic club where we swam at least once every week. He was a big man and handsome in a beefy sort of way and almost always had a pleasant smile. He could get into the spa after our swims and no matter who else was in the tub, he'd have them all in a good mood in no time at all. He just loved people and he needed to be loved. It was the same at the golf course. Playing golf with him, you'd feel happy no matter how bad a round you played. That's how infectious he was.

We both lived in Manhattan Beach just down the coast about thirty minutes on the 405 from Santa Monica where he had a high tolerance machining company that supplied Pentagon subcontractors all over Los Angeles with small parts for war machines from fighter jets to submarines and missiles. He was making a bundle, but he worked tirelessly for it. I was surprised he had energy for his swims and weekend golfing. We golfed at the Alondra course a few miles east of Manhattan Beach where I worked at nearby El Camino Community College, teaching English.

He could beat me in the pool, but I showed him the way around the golf course, although his beefiness occasionally connected perfectly off the tee, and he'd hit a straight ball to the 300-yard marker, sometimes more. But other than those few occasions, his game usually came in nearing 100 for a round while I rarely failed to break 85, especially at Alondra which was a relatively easy, flat public course with wide fairways.

We discovered we lived only two miles apart, but his place was in the pricey Hill Section on the southwest part of town, whereas I lived in a more modest part of east Manhattan Beach, a mile east of Highway 101 which had appreciated beyond the means of most middle-class Americans in the past twenty-five years. My wife and I couldn't afford our house if we had to buy it now. We had difficulty just trying to meet the yearly property taxes. But my salary had been continually bumped up with some good raises over the years, compliments of the California College System. Also, what we saved in state-provided comprehensive health insurance contributed to our privilege of being able to still afford Manhattan Beach.

The first time I saw Eliot's large ultra-modern home in the Hill Section at the beach was by his invitation to come over to watch the televised Masters golf tournament from Atlanta, Georgia. On Manhattan Avenue with the rear of the house facing out on the Pacific, his home took my breath away. The broad interior of contiguous living room, dining, and kitchen areas I estimated at around 2000 square feet. An infinity pool off the back patio of the house underlined a full view of the Pacific

Ocean from the living area where Eliot and I watched the Masters golf tournament that day. His luxurious house reminded me that lots of Pentagon dollars were flowing during those George W. Bush years, but I didn't begrudge Eliot, because he was a self-made man, and he didn't agree with attacking Iraq.

Tina and I had raised two kids in our modest three-bedroom stucco on Ruhland Avenue, put them through nearby Mira Costa High School and got them graduated from UCLA. We were both healthy and looking forward to grandchildren and a modest retirement. Tina's elementary school retirement plus mine would keep us well after retirement. But I suspected we'd have to downsize eventually, the greatly inflated value of our home being our largest investment account. Someday, we might want to move away from the Los Angeles area as many retirees were already doing to more affordable, healthier locations, sometimes out of state.

For Eliot and me, our economic positions had little influence on our friendship. He was rather impressed with my position as a college professor and my superior golf game, and I admired his business acumen and success. He had no vices, except for an occasional Cuban cigar. His avoidance of alcohol, I understood from his history of ten years with AA. We drank tea or soft drinks when we got together, although he went for Coca Cola if it was available. I suspected he had a mild sugar addiction, evidenced by a ready supply of Milky Ways and Kit Kats he kept in his golf bag. He'd often consume a chocolate bar after a swim at the club. After six months of our deepening acquaintance, swimming and golfing together, he invited me to bring my wife to his home for dinner.

Eliot's wife, Esther, was his second wife. He had two grown boys from his first marriage and had married Esther five years ago after he had cleaned up his act, as he described it.

"I was really a mess. I guess I'm still trying to make up for the heartache I caused my parents and my own kids. I was a runaround and a reckless drunk. My first wife divorced me which was no surprise and my boys disowned me. In retrospect, I never was truly in love with her. But she got pregnant, and I married her."

I praised how he had bounced back and made a great success of his life.

"Well, I owe it to the twelve-step and the kids who have since come around…slowly. And then meeting Esther totally renewed me. I fell completely in love with Essie. When I was younger, I didn't know diddly about love other than running around, you know what I mean, chasing skirts."

I did know what he meant. I'd had a checkered life before I met my wife, Tina. I have always insisted that she saved me. I think I would have wound up in a flop house somewhere living on SDI if I hadn't found her—or simply died an early death doing something stupid.

It was a Saturday night, the only night Eliot said he could really kick back. He had a partner, but it was all they could do with both their efforts to handle the rapid growth in the number of contracts. The Pentagon budget had grown, and it was being spent on a new generation of weaponry.

Eliot had poured off a couple glasses of Sauvignon Blanc for me and Tina, and he had popped open a flavored bubbly soda for himself while showing us around the house. Esther still hadn't made her appearance. He stopped at a wall where hung what I thought was an amateurish painting with nonsensical scribbles and wiggles which Eliot announced as his prize piece of art, an original Joan Miro. Esther had urged him to buy the painting at a small gallery auction in Paris. She knew art, and she insisted the Miro was a great investment. She had brought art into Eliot's life where there had been none before. He felt his life had been squandered up until he had met her. For their honeymoon she chose an art tour for them on the European continent, and she acted as his personal guide from the Netherlands and the Dutch Masters to France and the Fin de Siécle French iconic painters to Italy and the pantheon of the great Renaissance Italians such as Da Vinci, Raphael and Michelangelo. Professionally, Esther created artistic environments in rich people's homes, extravagant realizations of client dreams, often acknowledged in glossy design magazines. Just then the great artistic wife herself appeared.

Of course, it is the content of a person's character that matters, but there are times when appearances demand comments. Esther was a movie star grade beauty approaching mid-life, blonde, curvaceous, regal and finally, irresistibly charming. Her voice and accent echoed East-Coast aristocracy.

"I've heard a lot about you, the professor who plays golf like Arnold Palmer," she said, extending a hand to me.

"Eliot exaggerates." I replied. Next to his game, I felt like a master, but not Arnold Palmer. Eliot was powerful but didn't possess the finesse needed to deal with the dicey, delicate lies and shots the game inevitably presented, including the absolute focus required for great putting.

Tina introduced herself to Esther and commented on

the pleasing aroma that emanated from the kitchen.

"Smells like you've prepared something with three Michelin stars," Tina said, always gracious in social situations.

"Oh no, that's Eliot. Among his many talents is cooking. He didn't tell me what he's making. He always likes to surprise."

"Glass of wine, Love?" Eliot solicited as he returned from the kitchen wearing an apron and holding an open bottle of wine.

"Yes, please, Darling," she replied, and he poured her a glass.

The four of us were in front of the ceiling-to-floor bay window which looked out on the patio and the broad infinity swimming pool and the panorama of the sun about to dip below the Pacific horizon.

"Sometimes, first thing in the morning, if it's not too cold, I like to dash from bed and dive in the pool," Esther said.

"That would be exhilarating, for sure," Tina commented.

I couldn't help thinking of Esther prancing through the house naked and diving into the glass-like water.

With heels she was taller than Eliot and me, her height exaggerated by her simple, cream-colored straight gown that reached down to her feet, her regal slender neck and bare shoulders highlighted by a choker of pearls. I could see how she had been a reinforcing, sobering influence on Eliot. We had gathered at the dining table amidst a buzz of light chit-chat about food, art and our occupations. Eliot, being a fine gentleman, zeroed in on Tina, as if her career in teaching children were heroic. Esther focused on me.

"So, you teach English at El Camino. Current literature, too, I presume?" I nodded. "What contemporary novelists do you like?"

"Tim O'Brien, Annie Proulx, Frank McCourt, Jane Smiley, Tobias Woolf, Michael Ondaatje. You want me to continue?" The list ought to make her retreat, I thought.

She made me feel like I had to validate my credentials or what was I doing in her important presence? So, I decided to be more personal with her.

"So, besides morning dips and interior design, what do you do, Esther?"

"I do what I like," she said nonchalantly and set her glass on the table. "Please, Eliot dear, a dash more wine, thanks," she said.

I simply nodded at her with a small smile, as if to say, *touché*.

The dinner Eliot had prepared was French lamb chops in Cognac Dijon cream sauce with a lemony medley of veggies and saffron pilaf on the side. All of us ate very slowly, punctuating our consumption with polite inquiries and witty comments. Eliot attended to the table like a waiter, putting down plates, serving courses, refilling glasses, and finally bringing out dishes of lemon granita, followed by liquor glasses of Napoleon brandy. Esther never moved from her seat. Eliot did it all. Occasionally I would cook and serve dinners to give Tina a break, but I had the impression that Eliot's cooking, serving and clearing the table were not exceptional but the rule. Esther sat without concern through the whole dinner like the Queen of Sheba and didn't lift a finger.

As an interior designer and consultant, Esther served the rich class of the south beach communities from Playa Del Rey to Palos Verdes. She helped people decorate who had neither the time, inclination nor the talent to create a tasteful, show piece environment in short order. But they had the money to afford Esther. She interviewed her clients to determine their tastes and showed them dozens of photos of interiors to get their reactions. Finally, she would work up basic sketches of the spaces they wanted made over and she'd go from there. She had some real illustrating ability, and she knew furnishings from the exotic to early American to sparse modern geometrics, this latter style preferred by those who barely lived in their high-priced homes and trotted around the globe to live in their other properties according to whim and the seasons.

Eliot apparently helped Esther a great deal, getting leads from realtors he knew who supplied the names of people who'd bought into pricey luxury homes in the southwest beach areas. Eliot researched outlets for bargain prices on high end brands of furnishings and he'd collected a list of contractors who did remodeling and painting. He was her detail person in every regard. I had no idea where he found the time. He was her consummate helpmate.

When Tina and I were driving home, we were still trying to collect our thoughts and we had little to say until Tina broke the silence.

"How very strange. Esther told me she never cooks. She never learned."

"I've heard a lot of younger women don't cook these days."

"She told me not cooking or cleaning were part of their marriage agreement."

"Why not? Why should she want to do menial tasks when they can afford domestic help?"

"That may be true but if Eliot doesn't always cook, he picks up take-out or they have something delivered. They don't go out to eat much, she told me."

"Eliot appears to like cooking."

"While you and Eliot were out by the pool smoking those awful Cuban cigars, she and I talked quite a bit. I got the impression she's a princess and grew up with everything and demands that of Eliot. She admitted she couldn't run her business without him. She has no time for all the details. She's an artist and a designer, she emphasized, not a businesswoman. So, Eliot takes care of most of the details of her interior design business. Where does he find the time?"

"You don't like her much, do you?"

"Well, I doubt we'll be meeting for coffee and girl talk."

"Aren't you glad I cook half the time and I clean a little, my own space anyway?"

"I usually like your cooking, but your cleaning isn't thorough."

"I can't help it. My bachelor years gave me bachelor standards."

"I like Eliot. He's genuinely warm and sweet, but there's something tragic there. Call it a woman's intuition."

The next time I saw Eliot, I could see he was tired. He said he seldom got more than five hours a night. He and Esther often watched a late-night movie in bed, but she would usually sleep in when he got up, showered, had some breakfast and coffee, and went off to work. Meanwhile the machining subcontracting had picked up and he and his partner were having to hire more machinists and add shifts to get the work done. I couldn't help noticing his laps at the club pool were slower than they'd ever been.

"You know, Eliot, you're not immortal. Lots of guys drop off at sixty. You're trying to do too much." I told him in all seriousness.

Sadly, his older business partner that summer had a

massive heart attack on the squash court and didn't survive, effectively doubling Eliot's workload at their machine shop. But this didn't stop him from keeping his busy schedule, nor his usual joyful outward manner. After a swim one afternoon, he explained he had to run downtown to pick up some special lighting fixtures Essie had ordered for a palatial interior she was designing in Hermosa Beach. Then he had to pick up an order of groceries for dinner he was cooking that evening. I told him he should have something delivered and give himself a break.

I had begun feeling more than my usual gratitude toward Tina every time she gave me a basket full of washed and folded clothes to put away in my dresser.

"Eliot, eat your heart out," I'd say and kiss Tina.

"Never mind, just sweep off the porch and when you get a moment would you please fix that gutter downspout. It rattles with the slightest wind."

I told Eliot he should have one of their occasional Mexican housekeepers do his wash and pressing instead of him doing it himself."

And he told me Essie complained if they had the hired help in the house too much. They made her feel uncomfortable. He said most of his stuff was wash 'n wear and didn't need pressing. The rest of his clothing he took to the cleaners.

Tina wondered with a touch of sarcasm if Eliot's domestics were young and pretty, and I explained that they were middle-aged and fat. Esther just didn't like having hired help around the house more than necessary. I didn't push the point I was thinking. Why couldn't he just drop off all his laundry at a service?

Eliot started missing weekly swims which was no surprise. Between his machine shop business, now double the load after the death of the partner, and his being a servant in his own house, he didn't have the energy to keep up.

The only full break he got was when Esther went off to visit family in the Hamptons, an old wealthy family whose ancestors went back to colonial times, so he told me. She was raised with money and attended a posh arts and sciences college in New York City where she was trained in interior design.

I met with Eliot for a round of golf at the Alondra course while Esther was away. It was a Saturday, so he wasn't worried about the business. He had a good shop foreman who was overseeing extra machining on Saturdays, and he'd paid a cleaning crew extra to do a big house cleaning, washing, and pressing of clothes and making trays of enchiladas and other entrees that could be frozen for later. He was also on vacation. When we played rounds before, he'd walk for the exercise and let the electric cart carry his clubs. This time he rode the cart with me. I could see dark circles forming under his eyes. He was tired. But I also noticed he'd slimmed down a bit. At the ninth hole and the usual snack break, he had a tap beer, the first I'd ever seen him drink.

"Isn't that a little risky for you considering your past."

"Only one, don't worry. It's not a problem," he said and smiled.

Eliot parred the 10th hole, despite the beer, but when he bent down to retrieve his ball from the cup, he slumped to a knee and his head drooped as though his neck had gone slack.

"I'm all right, just a momentary lightness in the head. Probably it's the beer," he said.

"Maybe you ought to get checked by your doctor."

"Nah, I just need a little more rest."

"Look, Eliot, don't bother with our swim this week. How about you come by for an early dinner at my place tonight, and then go home early and get a good night's sleep?"

"Are you sure? I don't want to put Tina to any trouble."

It was decided and Eliot would come to dinner. Tina and I had hoped to get to know him a little better. But it seemed that all he could do was talk about Essie this and Essie that. We were relieved when he excused himself not long after finishing dinner, Tina's famous Farfalle pasta with Broccoli, finished with anchovy paste, lemon, garlic, and olive oil was a simple but sumptuous meal.

A whole week passed, and I hadn't heard from Eliot. It was Saturday and I was in the mood for a round of golf, so I called him on his cell phone and got no answer. I had his business card, so I called the machining works in Santa Monica. An impatient man with an unfriendly tone answered.

"Caldwell Machine. Foreman Jake Dearborn here."

"May I speak to Eliot Caldwell, please."

"Who is this?" The tone was more agitated than before.

"John Cochran, a neighbor and friend in Manhattan Beach."

"I guess you don't know."

"Know what?"

"Mister Caldwell had a car accident on the Santa Monica 405 three days ago."

"So how is he? Is he all right?"

"He rolled his Porsche at the interchange."

"How is he?"

"He was in critical condition and taken to intensive care, but sadly he passed a day later. Sorry, I had to break the news, Mr. Cochran."

I didn't bother to thank him or say goodbye. I just quietly hung up. I packed a few things from my faculty office and headed home. I stopped at the liquor store near our place on Ruhland and picked up a bottle of Cabernet and a copy of the local paper. The Beach Reporter already had Eliot's story on the second page, *Noted Manhattan Beach resident dies in a car accident on the Santa Monica Interchange.*

I wanted to get home and have a couple glasses of wine before Tina got home, before reading more in the Reporter. I kept thinking about the incident at the golf course when Eliot stooped to get his ball from the cup and slumped. He'd been pushing too hard, trying to do too much. I wondered how Esther was getting her head around this. Could Eliot's fatal accident have been avoided?

The Cowgirl and the Mafioso

My wife Maureen had met Eva at the Clothes Horse second-hand shop where they found a mutual attraction. They were women who loved flipping their ensembles and constantly renewing their closets at the Clothes Horse which was a local mecca for fashionistas. Often clothes still had their new tags but could be bought for a tenth of their retail price at a boutique or department store. Maureen and Eva were like kids in a candy store. The two women got closer when they discovered they were going to the same naturopathic doctor in town, treating recalcitrant thyroid glands. Woo-woo doctors and their prescriptions for health were also in fashion like the clothes Maureen and Eva hunted for.

I met Eva early on when she stopped by our place to see Maureen one Saturday. She was a well-built, attractive and in her late 30s with a sparkling personality. After we got to know her and she became familiar with us, she was often funny with jokes a bit risqué like those of Joan Rivers. She lived nearby just beyond the city limit where she had several acres and a few horses.

"What do you say we go Good Will hunting today?" she asked Maureen. It was still the 90s and good deals for quality stuff could still be found at the Good Will store. Maureen gave me a questioning look.

"No problem. I'm helping Lisa with a school project today and then I've got correspondences to catch up on." Weekends were always busy for me because my weekdays were mostly full at Edward Jones brokerage, sorting the markets and adjusting portfolios for my clients. I liked to spend some daytime hours with our daughter who had just started high school. She had a good arm for softball, and I enjoyed giving her practice, playing rounds of catch.

I had known for some time that Maureen was lonely for a close woman friend. None of the women at our weekly ballroom event at the Elks warmed up to her. I knew it wasn't her because she was open and free as the wind, a once-upon-a-time flower child comfortable in her skin, gracious and giving. I only made one friend and I lost him in a boating accident a year ago. So, I was happy for Maureen that she seemed to have found a soul sister in Eva. In their early days, Eva had Maureen come out to her ranch and took her riding around the acreage. Eva gave her a copy of a photo of them on horseback taken by the eldest son—two beautiful ladies, grinning ear to ear, riding the countryside together. Eva had written an inscription on the photo, *Friends forever, Eva.*

Then Eva invited us over to the ranch one Friday evening and Aldo, her husband, made dinner. At first, I thought of him as a man after my own heart. He liked to cook. He had run a dinner house back in Jersey where he had met Eva who tended the bar. Her affability would have made her a natural behind a bar. She had worked in a lot of low-paying service jobs in her youth like my Maureen, both coming from family backgrounds where college wasn't emphasized. I had been groomed for college by my father, and I understood now how his constant emphasis helped assure that I went to college. So, I did the same with our daughter. Eva and Maureen would probably still be doing low-paying service jobs if they hadn't married men who could support them. Maureen and I were equals despite her lack of a college education. She read novels voraciously and had the ability to remember details. She kept our banking and books as if she were a certified public accountant and she kept our house clean and orderly.

I saw the disparity between Eva and Aldo. Whereas she could have been a contestant for Miss America, he was a short, plain little man with a Jersey accent and poor grammar. He was in the dubious business of used car sales and had a lot on 11th Street. But I couldn't deny his graciousness that Friday night when he served up his divine Italian Scampi, accompanied by a vintage Pinot Grigio. I could be amenable to our occasional dinner with the Bellinis, but I didn't see me bonding with Aldo, one on one. There was an opaque crudeness about him contrary to the easy open sincerity of his wife.

I got some confirmation of my hunches the night the Bellinis came to our house for dinner for the first time. It was a perfect seventy-five-degree summer evening, so we dined on the patio, and I barbequed ribs while Maureen made sides of coleslaw and corn on-the-cob. Aldo was subdued most of the evening, steadily drinking wine. He was different from the man I met on his home turf. The confident veneer of tough businessman had evaporated and was barely evident, and by the time he and Eva left our house, he was drunk, and Eva had to help him out to their car which she assured us she was going to drive. As drunks sometimes do, he got maudlin and tearful and kept on about how much he loved her and swore with a sob he couldn't take it if she left him. It was a pathetic display and uncomfortable for us, but that evening confirmed that he existed in a marriage in which he was insecure, quite the opposite of what he projected the first time I met him. I knew what insecurity was in love from when I was young and in a relationship with a beautiful woman with whom I never quite felt equal. Looking back, that period of my life now seemed ridiculous. Marriage to Maureen had cured me of my youthful insecurities, and I needed no convincing that I was unconditionally loved and worthy.

I got to fill in some blanks from what Eva had passed along to Maureen. As a young woman of 21, Eva had been impressed with Aldo, his new Porsche, his wining and dining her, and the confident restauranteur he'd shown her when they were dating. He had kept his crude side from her in those early days. She learned later that he liked going to nude dancer bars with his pals, and with time he began using crude sexual references with her and about other women in general. She learned that the more she went along with his crudities, she could manipulate him. Maureen confided to me that he often wanted fellatio, Italian foreplay, as Eva humorously called it, when he got back from of his nights out with pals. Aldo saw everything as a transaction, even their marriage, she intimated to Maureen. I had to wonder what kind of creation she had become in her years with Aldo. Eva confessed once when in one of her Joan Rivers moments that her new Jaguar was her reward for *blowjobs* well-performed and laughed. Eva was often explicit with Maureen about the rough side of her marriage, but in mixed company she was charming and generally modest, except when she had one too many drinks, which we noted was becoming more often.

Our third couples' event was at an Outback restaurant, a chain of alleged Australian eateries featuring big steaks. Aldo ate a huge 16-ounce bloody filet all by himself, convincing me, if I had any doubts, that he was indeed really and metaphorically a red-meat sort of guy.

"I gotta keep my strength up. The car lot busted my balls all week," he said.

Eva, for her part, also ate like a lumberjack, including a large whole onion whose layers were cut and petaled like a large dahlia flower, then battered, and deep-fried. After that she ate an 8-ounce filet mignon and a double-baked potato with sour cream and chives, all accompanied by two large stemware glasses of Pinot. She rounded out this amazing consumption of calories with a slice of triple-layered carrot cake for dessert. I had to wonder how she kept such a svelte figure with this kind of eating. This couldn't have been a frequent occurrence for either of them. I guessed that going out to restaurants for them held a special familiarity and comfort. After all, that was where they had begun as a couple. Many couples went out to change the routine. In their case, I thought restaurants had become a refuge where they would retreat regularly to maintain an otherwise difficult marriage. They didn't have to talk, just eat, and drink.

Maureen and I, on the other hand, went for the six-ounce steaks with salads, and we kept to a single glass of wine each. The light volume of our consumption had been conditioned by our frequent practice of ballroom dancing which maintained our fitness and we'd grown to eat less to keep trim for the dance. I could see where Aldo and Eva were headed if the Outback dinner experience became frequent.

Maureen and Eva were still going for their weekly horse rides at the ranch and along adjoining trails of county property. Maureen was enjoying emulating Eva's cowgirl getups of fitted Levi jeans, boots and Western style shirts she'd found at the Clothes Horse. I came home early after a short day one afternoon when Maureen and Eva had come back to the house after a couple hours in the saddle.

"Howdy, how y'all doing' there, pard?" Eva greeted me with her country impersonation as I came through the door. She was the picture of Marilyn Monroe in her last movie with Clark Gable but sounded like the hickish sidekick Thelma Ritter rather than the breathy Monroe. We all sat down and had coffee, and Eva reeled off some personal history.

"My granny had a homestead near Mobile, Alabama, raised chickens, had a few cows, churned homemade butter." When she first met Aldo and learned that he had a twin brother, she blurted out, *Your brother short like you?* We couldn't help laughing. This was a anecdote I was sure Aldo hated.

So, one of Eva's alter-ego characters was that of her grandmother on whom she fashioned an amusing answering message on her home phone which initially made me think of granny from the old Beverly Hill Billys' television show. Eva loved to entertain and be in the spotlight. For me, most memorable was her impersonation of two Southern Belles gossiping. One asked the other, *Is Elly Mae going to the hoedown with Bubba?* The other Belle replied, *I have no idea, Bobbi-Jo.* And BJ responds, *Don't you know? We don't talk to Elly Mae no mo.* And the first Belle was surprised and responded, *We don't? Why?* And on it went. I envisioned Eva successfully doing standup comedy at local clubs with her sexy good looks and her disparate southern hick impersonations. She was spontaneous, vivacious and great fun. No wonder Maureen bonded with her. So many women acquaintances Maureen had in town, including those in the so-called Ballroom Community, were ultimately closed off and socially inept with little to share or no sense of humor.

Our next foursome dinner with Eva and Aldo was at Giannini's Trattoria. It had been several weeks since we'd last seen them. The svelte Eva was suddenly packing on the pounds and Aldo was a bit more round. They were more subdued than usual. Aldo was complaining about too many auto repossessions. What did he expect? He let just about anyone buy a car on time, no questions asked. He then surprised me and Maureen just as we were finishing our first glass of Chianti. Eva was already working on her second glass which Maureen noted to me with a frown.

"I just send over my pal Louie 'The Hook' with his tow truck and his muscle Angelo, and no problem," he said and chuckled at me with an evil smirk.

"Don't let him bullshit you guys," Eva said, "he likes to think he's some sort of West Coast Mafia."

"Yeah, that's right and I'm taking my orders direct from Don Corleone in Jersey," Aldo said, and chuckled some more.

He was joking, of course, but there was something disturbing in his manner, as if he took glee in repossessions, a drastic sort of legal action that for many poor struggling people had painful consequences. I had never forgotten my friend Barney in college who begged the thuggish repossession men who came to take away his Volkswagen. He pleaded with them at 2 am one night to let him keep his car one more day while he got money from the bank to make a late payment. They were deaf to his pleas.

Riding horses and dinners out were nice, but the girls wanted to step out for an evening, maybe until ten or so, by themselves without their men.

I had no objections. I was happy for Maureen who was tickled to have a congenial girlfriend she could step out with for an evening. It meant looking pretty, protecting each other and having a few drinks. That was where I stepped in. I knew Maureen was prudent about driving but I wasn't so sure about Eva, so I insisted Maureen drive for the evening. Eva for her part agreed but she would drive in from the outskirts of town to our place and go from there. Fine. If Eva got too tipsy, they would have an evening snack and a Café Americano at our place before she drove back to the ranch.

When Maureen dolled up, she was magnificent with her huge shock of graying curly hair and a little shadow around the eyes that put her in a league with Betty Davis, only much softer. Her outfit was lacey conservative, but chic and she wore medium height heels with a straight black skirt. Eva arrived at the appointed time and briefly stepped into the doorway. She had on a skirt that left little to the imagination, outlining her curves like a mermaid without the fishtail. She had on a suitable light shrug for a wrap but her bustline was plainly framed. She must have worn a push-up bra because her cleavage was hard not to notice. And she wore stiletto heels. She had her hair taken up for a change that saved her from looking decidedly cheap. She hadn't overdone her makeup, so her facial contours were subtly emphasized, taking the edginess off her overall appearance. She looked uptown instead of downtown. Maureen, a few years older than Eva, appropriately looked like the older, attractive sister.

They had gone to the pricey Hilton Hotel bar, had a couple weak drinks, which is what the Hilton served at high prices, and they came back to our place around 11 pm, happy for the experience. I could only imagine it was their making an appearance as if available desirable women garnering looks that made them feel good. That they could sit at a bar and chat for two and half straight hours made me happy for Maureen because she'd finally found herself a soulmate lady friend.

The next morning Maureen got an early call from Eva. Would Maureen please come and meet her at Peace Health Hospital on 13th Street? She needed Maureen's help. She would say no more. But muffled sobs were heard. I was at my office when Maureen called to let me know that Aldo in a jealous rage had assaulted Eva and that she was in bad shape. She was getting treated but according to the attending physician she would need surgery to correct the damage done to her face. Maureen had offered to bring her to our place, but Eva insisted on recovering at Women's Space, a local organization dedicated to battered women. When she was back on her feet, she was going to get a small apartment and a lawyer. Women's space recommended lawyers who were especially known for their toughness with wife-beating spouses.

Aside from bruises and swelling, and a closed black eye, Eva had sustained a fractured orbital bone and a broken nose, and cuts to her upper lip. Those things would heal with time, but the injury to her mind perhaps never. Aldo had kept her awake most of the night with his rabid accusations and his doubts about her faithfulness, finally slapping her hard with his left hand and then taking her down with a right-handed punch. She was able to get dressed and drove immediately to the hospital and filed a complaint with the police and two officers came to Emergency to interview her. She gave them her address, but she wouldn't return to the house.

Aldo was arrested and carted off to jail, according to the law. He subsequently had his lawyer bail him out the following morning, and upon appearing in court for his case was convicted of only a misdemeanor and required to pay a $6500 fine, all hospital bills, and $15,000 in damages to his battered wife, all which Aldo easily paid without any pain.

Her attorney wanted her to press with more severe charges but either she developed guilt, as some battered women do, or she believed if she went easier on Aldo, he would make a more generous settlement.

Maureen found out Eva didn't have her name in joint ownership of anything. Apparently, she had made no legal prenuptial agreement with Aldo. As Maureen concluded, Eva had been young, impressionable, and lacked foresight when she married Aldo.

To me, Aldo had put one over on the young Eva. He'd made sure he had an open back door in his marriage. Poor, young Eva with stars in her eyes hadn't had enough savvy to insist on a toe hold on some property and now she had to rely on his generosity—when he had no generosity toward her, nor compassion. He was a repossession man, after all.

Maureen saw Eva a few times in the months after the incident as she recovered from her injuries and surgeries. Maureen said that every time she saw Eva, she was drinking. Then Eva disappeared without notice. We weren't about to call Aldo to ask where. Aldo was also gone. The ranch had been sold along with the horses, and we didn't know what was going to happen to their boys. How could poor Eva care for them by herself anyway? I got chills thinking about the oldest boy of 10 who had an uncanny resemblance to Aldo.

For weeks after the incident, I felt bad for Eva. I was relieved I hadn't run into Aldo in town and done or said something rash. What was there to talk about? The used car lot on 11th Street displayed a big sign announcing an under-new-management sale.

I still occasionally think of Eva, the cowgirl, and remember how funny she was and how sad her circumstances became. As for Maureen, she has long since traded in her Western riding duds at the Clothes Horse second-hand shop. Ever optimistic, Maureen said she still hoped to find a soul sister friend to round out her life, and I consoled her with a hug and suggested that next time she found a candidate, she better check out her other half.

Long Ago and Far Out

In the latter half of the 60s, we were doing so much marijuana, we'd gone down the rabbit hole. It was the beginning of an illegal culture that is now legal with more marijuana shops in town than convenience stores. The war in Viet Nam was deepening while popular music called us to rebel. I was a graduate student at California State College of Long Beach which provided me with a deferment from the war and a continuation of the good times and not having to make hard decisions. A lot of colleges in that era were like ours, centers of political unrest, marijuana, promiscuity, and wonder. We raised a cry for freedom, but we weren't conscious of how much freedom we already enjoyed, taking our privileged Californian lives for granted.

My friend Bob McGrath had worked hard through school to become a hotshot lawyer who was hired into the firm of Stanley Fleishman and Associates in Hollywood, famous for defending porn and other first amendment issues. But he'd had no time for travel or youthful adventures. Being involved in dealing pot, insomuch as I could gather, and hanging out with hip people gave him a sense of being part of the flamboyant counterculture. In short, he wanted to be cool.

"After all," he questioned, as if giving a summation to a jury, "is the Establishment reaction to pot any different from the Twenties' prohibition of alcohol? At least weed doesn't kill like booze, right?"

Of course. It seemed excessive to impose prison terms for possession of a little innocuous marijuana. McGrath knew better than anyone that dealing quantities of marijuana could get you a stiff prison sentence. But like all of us, he didn't see using it as morally wrong, and somebody had to supply the extensive public demand. You just had to be careful. In fact, pot was conducive to peace and love. All of us felt that pot was a great contribution to changing the world for the better. Didn't world peace hero John Lennon extol the virtues of pot?

I met McGrath at the Bearded Clam, a pub and dance hall down in Huntington Beach on the Pacific Coast Highway where I occasionally played bass for a local rock group. We fell into talking about the Beat poets and Aldous Huxley, things I'd read while going for a Master of Fine Arts degree. My hair had grown to my shoulders which I often wore in a ponytail, but McGrath had to keep his hair business short and wear suits and ties. He admired that I had traveled and spoke Spanish, which was my minor throughout my undergrad days rounded out by a year of travel in Mexico.

"How would you like to make a nice chunk of quick cash?" he asked one night when we were out on the Palos Verdes peninsula overlooking the Pacific and enjoying the sea air and a joint of Acapulco Gold. He lived up there because he'd found a cheaply priced house damaged by earthquake tremors and most likely sitting on unstable ground. He had an odd attractive wife named Melissa who wore thick glasses with strong magnification making her eyes appear freakishly big. She was as curious a character as his unexpected offer of a chunk of cash. What poor student like me wouldn't have been interested?

"We're negotiating some deals down in Tijuana that involve a quantity of weed."

"We?"

"Investors."

"How much weed?"

"A hundred kilos of premium Acapulco Gold. With so much money and product involved we can't miss anything in translation, so we want you at the table helping us keep things clear. I'm talking one evening of your time, the ride down to Tijuana, an hour or so with the Mexicans and the ride back. What do you say?"

"How much are you going to pay me?"

"Three hundred after we have possession of the weed."

"How about the money before going to Tijuana?"

I knew he had no backup guy. You can't just bring in anybody to the kind of deal they were planning. It had to be somebody close that was trusted. McGrath didn't want to pay up front, but I insisted, and he didn't dig his heels in because he couldn't. They needed me, and soon. The other investors in league with McGrath turned out to be Rob Norris and The Artsy Boutique shop partners in Belmont Shore, Joe Dugan and Danny Petersen, all people I knew. The caper had formed without my knowing, but then I guessed they realized they finally had to bring me in with my Spanish ability for a bit of added security. When I questioned McGrath why I hadn't been asked to participate earlier, he explained that the need for somebody who knew Spanish was an afterthought for some security.

"We all knew you didn't have money to invest, so there was no need to discuss the caper with you."

"Gee, I'm glad you decided you could use me." I felt compelled to add a little sarcasm.

"We just figured the less you knew the better if the caper went down badly. You wouldn't be implicated."

"Nice to know you were looking out for me."

"Okay then, see me tomorrow afternoon and I'll give you the cash. And now you're in it, brother."

"Thanks, I could use the money." I was always broke.

"Far out," McGrath said, and we shook hands.

Rob Norris, one of the three conspirators, the unkempt one, was overweight with stringy black hair, a working-class intellectual who was stoned every evening after work for lack of hobbies, other than listening to his high-powered reel-to-reel tape sound system. He dealt a little because other than rent for his large apartment on west Second Street, he spent his money on wholesale purchases of premium pot. And according to McGrath, Norris was an eager investor when the Tijuana caper came up. I remember dropping by Norris's place one weekend and being introduced to The Moody Blues whose wistful, ethereal song, *Nights in White Satin,* seemed to describe Rob's lonely, loveless existence. But we could get loaded together and find something to laugh about. And now and then I'd buy a little dope from him which was always high quality and reasonably priced.

Joe Dugan and his partner Danny Petersen, who owned the artisan candle shop that also sold handmade hippie goods of every description on Second Street in Belmont Shore, comprised the other leg of the investing triumvirate and the source of the plan to smuggle a large quantity of marijuana across the border from Tijuana. It turned out they had been dealing for quite a while. Their Artsy Boutique shop was a convenient front where cars could drive into the rear receiving garage to be unloaded.

I had known Danny from high school, where he'd been two years behind me and his older sister Caroline. He was a clean-cut, short-haired, studious looking kid who you'd never suspect was running a major marijuana operation. Joe, on the hand, was often unshaven, scruffy and sleazy. He seemed always ready with a comment on the newest soft porn cinema like *I am Curious Yellow* which was being hyped as high art at pretentious art house theaters. He often gleefully referenced John Holmes, the famous porn actor of the time and his giant cock. I heard that Dugan could be a tough customer. He dealt with the secondary tier of dealers who made small purchases of two or three kilos which they in turn retailed in one-ounce baggies to college kids and others around Long Beach and adjacent towns. Dugan had been up in Bellflower closing a deal one evening with three Cholo toughs who made the mistake of messing with him, and it ended with Joe leaving all three hurting and prone in a parking lot, the pot they'd purchased scattered all over the asphalt. The story had made it to the local paper. Joe wasn't identified or mentioned, while the Bellflower lads took the fall, getting arrested for possession when the cops arrived at the pot-strewn scene minutes after the altercation.

Joe and Danny were in for fifty percent of the pot shipment and McGrath and Rob Norris in for twenty-five percent apiece as silent partners. I learned that they took a pound of stash for themselves in addition to their original investments plus a share of the profit, but McGrath and Norris kept their distance from the actual execution of the caper and the subsequent dealing.

The pot scene was tame in those days compared to what it became by the 70s. The Tijuana negotiation seemed more like a warm cooperative than the dangerous dope deals we now see portrayed by Hollywood. There were no guns or surly gangster types present and the Mexicans were a decent, accommodating lot. Danny, Joe, and I were at the table across from the two Mexicans whose main spokesman introduced himself as Jorge, who was from Guadalajara where I had spent several months of my year in Mexico when I was an undergraduate. So, we struck up a little rapport. We just had to agree how we were going to get the grass to Long Beach and how they were going to get paid. I helped oil the exchanges with a little Spanish that, if nothing else, made the Mexicans feel a little more relaxed. It was agreed the Mexicans would get the marijuana across the border as they had so often done. They had a grandmother with two grandchildren in the back seat of an old lumbering '54 Lincoln Capri, ostensibly going to visit her relatives in San Diego, a common situation among Mexican nationals living in Tijuana.

The border in those days was much more porous, and dope-sniffing dogs hadn't yet been employed. Pot wasn't yet seen as a big American problem. Mexican suppliers weren't cartel controlled at that time and border control was light. Tijuana was still a popular weekend destination for Americans tourists, including sailors from the San Diego naval base, who mostly came for the gambling and girlie shows. After about an hour with the Mexican dealers, we left the meeting house off the main drag, Revolution Street, and headed to the border. It was still early, about eight pm.

"While we're here, you guys, let's stop in for a show at the Blue Fox," Joe suggested.

In those days, The Blue Fox was Tijuana's legendary girlie show bar, a popular destination for college boys and sailors from the San Diego Naval base.

"Sorry, Joe, I'm driving us back. We came down for business, remember?" Danny was always more business-like than Joe, perhaps because he had a degree in business administration from Long Beach State.

"My deal didn't include hanging out in Tijuana beyond the negotiations. So, let's get back to Long Beach pronto," I said.

Later that week, the Mexican grandmother driver arrived in San Diego, and the Mexican plates on the '54 Lincoln Capri were changed to California plates. Two Anglo-looking Mexicans took over the driving to Long Beach and into the rear receiving garage of the Artsy Boutique shop where the concealed grass was removed from the vehicle. First, the Mexicans counted out the $20,000 that came in 20 stacks of twenty-dollar bills and then got to work tearing down the Lincoln. I was amazed at how the marijuana was concealed in the seats, door panels, the car ceiling, behind the dash and in the spare tire compartment. Then the Lincoln was jacked up and a suitcase sized metal container was unbolted from the undercarriage of the car which had most of the bricks. If indeed the pot had high quality, the retail street value would quadruple what was paid to the Mexicans. When all the dope was removed, they put the Lincoln back together, while Joe and Danny weighed out the marijuana. When the car was reassembled and the pot weighed out as expected, the Mexicans bid us adios and backed the Lincoln out of the garage and left, presumably for Tijuana.

Joe and Danny gave me eight ounces as a bonus, a lot of personal stash to me, not a regular user. After all, I had an MFA project to complete, some part-time work clerking at a liquor store, and occasionally I stood in with a local rock band on bass. McGrath was happy to collect his investment back and a bonus stash of dope. Norris was equally happy with his return. It was Joe and Danny who were having to work hard to unload so much dope wholesale, although they had a list of well-heeled, trusted buyers.

A week after the drop, some complaints trickled down. Danny told me he thought the lot had been cut with common grade dope. It certainly wasn't a hundred percent Acapulco Gold. Unfortunately, dope deals didn't allow for returns or exchanges like a purchase from Sears. *Caveat emptor.* I noticed the stash I'd been given had begun to show some unevenness in the highs it produced, but I wasn't the connoisseur that Joe and Danny were. Breaking open some of their bricks and testing, they concluded their fears were true. The bricks had been packed in their cores with medium grade dope and then given an outer layer of high-grade stuff. Unfortunately, Joe and Danny were still holding a lot of the original shipment. Most of the kilo brick buyers discovered the subterfuge and demanded part of their money back and Joe and Danny obliged, wanting to retain their steady customers. Joe, Danny, McGrath, and Norris managed to recoup almost all their original cash investments over a couple months despite the scam.

When trying to get rid of the remaining bricks, Joe and Danny became loose, fronting kilos to people to deal for commission. Joe offered me a cache of five kilos to deal for a 30 percent commission, but I turned him down. I had no interest in hustling sales. Many single lid buyers were content to buy dime bags of mixed quality dope that made joints you could smoke down without getting floored, nothing like pure Acapulco Gold that was a lot stronger. So, the next tier of buyers down from Danny and Joe had to make some unexpected adjustments in their sales.

While the pot deal's fallout was being resolved, my nephew Tim from Downey showed up at my apartment. He'd just turned 17 and was putting on a show for me, his senior by a decade. He was almost a man but not filled out yet. He was tanned and athletic looking with real blond hair that underscored his identity as a surfer. My older brother Gary could be generous and had helped him finance a 1952 two door, stick shift sedan and Timmy decided to drive over from Downey to impress me.

"Hey, Uncle, I just thought it would be cool to drive down and see what you're up to. We only get bits about you now and then from dad."

I used to visit my older brother Gary now and then when I was younger, but I hadn't been over to Downey much in recent years during college. Unfortunately, my brother had strangely become enamored with Governor Ronald Reagan, an adversary of the working class and a proponent of right-to-work laws. I didn't get it. Gary's AFL-CIO machine shop union had been his protector and benefactor for years. Gary had married just out of high school and had Timmy and then two more kids. Since I started college, Gary and I haven't had much to talk about.

"Well, I'm finishing college which is where you ought to go next year after you graduate high school. How about nearby Cerritos City College, it's free?"

"How do you like my far-out wheels, even a nice roof rack for my Hobie." Timmy wasn't paying any attention.

"Cool, Tim, very cool." I didn't want to pop Tim's jubilant bubble. My old Chevy wasn't a whole lot better than his Ford jalopy.

"I've been promised a machining trainee job when I graduate."

It was clear Tim wasn't going to college, but I made no further issue and just smiled. He was an intelligent kid, naïve and vulnerable like everyone at his age. I surmised that Tim wasn't getting encouragement to go to college at home. That was ironic but credible. When Gary and I were growing up, our old man had often stressed the importance of getting an education, and he was disappointed in my older brother's choices. But then Gary and the old man never got along very well.

"Hey, Uncle, how would you like to smoke a doobie with me?"

Timmy pulled out a fat joint from his pocket and without waiting for my answer, fired it up.

"What in the hell are you doing?!"

"What does it look like?"

"You're too young to be smoking that shit."

"So, what's the big deal about smoking a little marijuana?"

"Look, how about you put that thing out and we have a little coffee and some sober talk?"

Tim was agreeable, and I began making some instant Medaglia d' Oro expresso with milk and sugar.

"I know you don't want to hear this but you're still a growing kid, well, young man, and pot is just going to scramble your brain before it's fully developed. Where do you get your weed, anyway?"

"It's everywhere, man. There're guys at school who deal out of their lockers. Don't you smoke?"

"Of course, sometimes, but not often. I mean, like there's other things that have to get done. How often do you smoke?"

"Like almost every day, sort of."

I couldn't help thinking that his school's student dealers may have been selling stash from the Tijuana shipment I was associated with. After all, Downey was only fifteen miles from Long Beach.

"Look, Timmy, too much of this stuff is a one-way ticket to becoming a dope. Smoking regularly is going to fry your brain," I said and handed him a cup of coffee.

"So, I'll cut back. School is so boring; a little smoke is a relief. I can hardly wait to graduate and just do my own thing."

The image of a grinning Rob Norris passed before me, his sweaty print shop existence all day long, every week, and his brain-numbing smoking of pot every evening. Approaching forty, Norris was neither growing nor going anywhere—like running in place.

"Let's ease off the serious talk. Come on, I'll take you to see a matinee for some laughs and a box of popcorn."

The kid had arrived at my doorstep with a smile and warm intentions. I didn't want to make his rare visit a drag. So, I decided to take him to see the movie, *Dr. Strangelove or How I Stopped Worrying and Love the Bomb*. Maybe Kubrick's brilliant new satire that would startle him a bit into asking questions and give him something to think besides surfing, girls, and pot.

I knew Bob McGrath didn't smoke during his days while he had to sort briefs and defend clients in court. He was on the cusp of becoming a partner in his law firm. Joe and Danny were enjoying their stalled youth and the hedonistic times, running their hippy-dippy art store and dealing dope. But at least they had an investment they were nurturing. They didn't waste days stoned. Danny even kept a set of meticulous books, one for the store and one for the pot they were dealing. Joe stayed straight when dealing or working in the store, so he too wasn't a big user and mainly used his constant supply of dope to entice liberated college women. A lot of users wanted us to believe pot wasn't addictive, but using every day was an addiction.

I wasted too much time in a cloud of marijuana smoke back in the day, a time when I might have turned thoughts and dreams into action. But fortunately, by the time I got into my early-thirties, I tired of smoking pot as well as tobacco, serial monogamy, and California in general. I cut my hair short and left for back East, married a sensible, well-read woman out of Barnard College and luckily found a solid teaching job where I eventually got tenured.

But I can't forget my pot-fueled, dreamy twenties in Long Beach, that sweet bird of youth. I am sad to learn about my once handsome, blond surfer nephew Timmy, now an old man like me, who had become a case of lost potential, minimally educated with a spotty work history of hand-to-mouth jobs, now living in penurious retirement. I am told he has found Jesus and Donald Trump and has all the answers. Gratefully, I haven't heard from him. His Christian evangelism, I am told, at least saved him from the abject depths of drugs and alcohol use. One of Tim's adult children on Facebook, who has been a source of information about my extended family in California, informed me that Tim regularly goes to a local Christian mission in Oxnard, California where he now lives and holds meetings for the homeless, aspiring to show them the path to Jesus and salvation. Tim had managed to have a couple marriages in his younger years and produced four children who sadly haven't risen above his life's stunted example, except for one, my Facebook contact, who had developed a thriving plumbing business. My brother Gary prematurely passed away twenty years ago of liver cirrhosis.

I've often wondered what became of the unkempt Rob Norris. I'm sure it was sad and lonely and probably fraught with diabetes or emphysema if he'd lived so long. Bob McGrath, on the other hand, is most likely retired from a profitable career in the law and is probably taking posh European river cruises or living and playing golf in the tony desert community of Rancho Mirage.

A few years ago, I met Danny Petersen's sister Caroline at my 50th high school reunion that I flew out to Los Angeles to attend, and she told me her brother Danny was living in Bangkok with a Thai woman, trying to dry out from alcohol. All I know of Joe Dugan is what I learned from an old acquaintance I ran across on Facebook who is still living in Long Beach. He wrote he'd recently seen Dugan on Belmont Shore's busy Second Street, clean-shaven and dapper, strolling arm in arm with an attractive woman who looked half his age.

The One-Eyed Girl

I didn't know what I was doing, drinking glass after glass of Beef Eater gin with tonic. I was an inexperienced kid, and it was my first time drinking hard liquor and it just tasted like interesting pop with a wedge of lime. I was at Phil Rigby's architectural summer house on a bluff overlooking the Pacific and a Carlsbad beach cove. Rigby and John English kept telling me to slow down, but Rigby kept setting them up anyway.

Up until then when I had just turned nineteen, I had never been drunk, nor had I ever been so sick. I had to walk on the beach for a whole day and I couldn't eat, and I only drank water. I had been poisoned, but my position as a young friend to Rigby and John English had been established, although at an exacting price. These older guys impressed me. I discovered that Phil Rigby, in his early forties and already balding and overweight, was a scion of the famous Rigby real estate clan who owned huge swaths of Southern California coastal land. John English was a handsome, burly rugby star going into his senior year at UCLA that coming fall.

It was the summer of 1959, and I had a summer job at the Carlsbad Army/Navy academy summer camp for boys. John English was head lifeguard and responsible for all the beach activities. I was one with three others who oversaw land activities and acted as older brothers to one hundred younger campers. We also had some rotating waterfront duties. Our presence seemed to be our most important function and I had a lot of free time. The camp facilities consisted of a large u-shaped string of rooms like a motel where the campers were housed, and I occupied a corner room. My associate counselors occupied the other strategic corners of the resident quad. Just beyond the quad were buildings that housed a pool, a basketball court, an auditorium, a large dining hall and the administrative offices. A football field and track were on the other side of Highway 101 from the school grounds. Most campers came from well-off families and were well-behaved.

If we had a discipline problem, we were required to report it immediately and the administration dealt with the occasional unruly camper with military efficiency. It was an easy summer job, a vacation really, with pay. We had to organize and run a few things such as a volleyball competition on the beach, a track meet, ping pong and chess tournaments.

But during the long hot summer, the beach was always the center of activity. The water was clean then and often had enough good waves to allow for some moderate surfing. On a flat part of the beach where the water rolled up, leaving a thin layer of water, skim boarding was popular. We counselors were given instructions to do our best to impress campers with the value of using sunscreen. The administration didn't want any kids with sunburns. On that point they may have been ahead of their time. We enforced a strict buddy system on the water in which campers could only go out into the water in pairs as a safety measure.

John English would sit up on his lifeguard tower like a blond, bronze god with his aviator sunglasses, watching over the camp's designated beach. When he saw someone making some infraction of the rules, he'd blow his whistle and call out the camper with his bullhorn. I spent a lot of time at the beach that summer and acquired the best tan of my life. It was also the most I'd ever surfed.

Louise appeared on the beach one afternoon when I was taking a break and just enjoying deepening my tan. John English wanted us counselors out on the waves to lend example and help if needed. I was just coming out of the water with my surfboard when Louise and I intersected.

"Nice board," she said, and she stopped to let me pass.

"You surf?" I asked.

"I can. I live just up the beach," she said with a wave of her hand in the direction of the Rigby enclave of classy beach homes. I was trying to redirect my attention away from the eye patch she was wearing. She had long blondish hair with a wave that fell across the patch. Otherwise, she was young and magnificent in her well-fitted, white one-piece swimsuit that contrasted with her dark tan that matched the color of the eyepatch.

"I'm really not playing pirate," she said, grinning and gesturing to her patch."

"What happened?"

"Cancer!"

She was dead serious, and I felt a chill run up my body and a flush starting around my ears.

"Yep, lost the eye! Better to keep it covered. What's left ain't pretty. I know, you're shocked. Everybody is."

I felt something more than shock. I felt a sudden sorrow and pity for someone so young and beautiful. Louise Paxton lived in one of the modern beach homes on the bluff in Rigby's neighborhood. She'd just graduated from Carlsbad High School in June, and she was in remission. I had the sense that she'd found her condition had given her a special power in everyday social contacts. She confounded whomever she met. She was blonde, slender, pretty, and deeply tanned. But cruelly flawed.

She guessed that I worked for the summer camp. She knew all about it. She'd lived at that part of the Carlsbad beach most of her young life. Of course, she was familiar with the regular school year at the Army/Navy academy. She said she never much cared for it, that there were a lot of strange boys during the regular school year from autocratic foreign countries being prepped to become generals. She wanted to go to UCLA and study medicine where she'd been successfully treated for her rare condition.

"I've applied and I expect I'll be accepted. I have the grades and the UCLA Medical Center wants me nearby to monitor my condition."

I told her about my track scholarship to Pepperdine college in Los Angeles. I had been a top Bay League high school sprinter, and although I was expected to win the league title, having beaten all my rivals in dual meets, I came in third in the finals because of a sore ham string. Anyway, my athletic laurels helped me get my position at the summer camp, directing sports activities and being a big brother counselor to the younger campers.

Louise and I were rolling along with exchanges when John English paged me on his bullhorn from the lifeguard tower. Louise said she'd look for me again as she had the habit of walking a mile or two along the water most days.

John was upset with me because I wasn't keeping my eye on surfing campers while chatting with Louise. "I don't always see everything from up here."

"When the kids catch a big wave, keep your eyes peeled for wipeouts who don't pop back up as soon as they should."

"Sorry, John. You're right. I was taking a short break."

"Find some other time to chat up nutty Louise."

"You know her?"

"Everybody does. She lives here," English said, pointing up the beach.

My brief meeting with Louise at the water's edge had awakened in me a frisson of desire. Girls had been on hold for me since I'd been at the camp with its all-male, sports-oriented environment. My experience with girls then was as developed as my experience with alcohol. Nevertheless, I resented John English referring to her as *crazy*. She was quite sane and poised toward me. But his comment stuck in my mind as I hoped to run into Louise again on the beach.

The sunny days passed by quickly, and I was assigned to organize an all-camp track meet on the athletic field across the 101. The facility with showers and lockers at one end of the field became my headquarters. I had help from one of the other counselors, like me a recent high school graduate named Dallas Boone who'd been an all-CIF halfback at Downey High School in Los Angeles. We had several camper helpers, organizational types, who liked sports but didn't participate, usually the academic high-achievers and chess guys. The administration provided us with ribboned medals for first, second and third in each event. The gold first place medals were only plated, but all the medals were top quality and looked as good as any I had from my track career in high school.

For two weeks in the runup to the meet, I was almost always at the field, over-seeing kids training and readying themselves for the meet. Dallas was clocking kids working on the mid-distance races. I was showing kids how to use the starting blocks for sprints and the real form for getting over low hurdles. We even held a mile run, four times around the quarter-mile track and a lot of tall, lean kids sign up. Dallas and I excluded the pole vault because neither of us had any experience with the event and no one seemed to notice or ask for it. A lot of kids signed up for the long jump and the sprints. The quarter-mile relay got a lot of enthusiastic participation because of the four-man team effort required.

Saturdays were open and so I got some time at the beach without having to monitor the surf under the watchful eyes of John English. I kept to the further end of the camp's designated beach in the direction of the rich enclave where I thought I might run into Louise. She didn't appear that first Saturday, but she did the next. Dallas had joined me for a little round of catch with a football and pretended plays with quarterback to receiver, which was easily done without the pressure of an opposing defensive safety. Dallas was a talented broken-field runner and had huge hands able to pull in one-handed catches. He had a wide pleasant face and was as personable and softly spoken as he was a talented football player headed to either Notre Dame or Southern Cal.

When Louise came down the beach, this time wearing a canary-yellow one-piece swimsuit and matching eye patch. She approached with a big smile and asked if she could join in throwing the football. What young men would say no to such a pretty, damaged girl? Surprisingly, she easily caught a soft floater I threw her, but her throwback didn't have nearly the same grace with which she'd caught the ball. I threw to Dallas, and he also threw Louise a soft floater she could catch easily. But then she suddenly took off with the ball and started to run away down the beach, laughing and hooting as she went. Dallas and I looked at each other in surprise and then grinning, we started after her. Of course, we caught up with her easily, which she no doubt intended. We did our best to be gentle. Dallas grabbed for the ball when he got close, but Louise artfully stepped away. Then I reached in and snatched the ball from her, and when she reached out to snatch it back, a sharp nail raked my torso just to the right of my navel, leaving a deep vertical scratch of about three inches.

"Goddamn it, Louise, look what you've done!" I yelled at her. The scratch stung and my anger flared, and blood streamed from the wound. The rowdiness and laughter ceased and Dallas took possession of the ball.

"Let's go to the lifeguard tower, there's a first aid kit. We'll clean you up," he said. Now my hand covering the scratch had turned crimson with the flow from the gash.

"Damn it, Louise, trim your nails if you're going to play rough," I said with restrained anger. She apologized several times, insisting it was just an unfortunate accident. It was, of course, but I still felt angry.

At the lifeguard tower, when we told English what had happened, he responded, "That girl is trouble."

Then he got out his first aid kit and treated the wound, cleaning it with a cotton swab and hydrogen peroxide and for good measure gave it a coat mercurochrome. He taped on a cotton patch and gave me some extra dressings and told me to keep it clean and dry and stay out of the water for a few days.

"The less you guys have to do with that girl, the better," English said as we left the lifeguard tower.

I carried around a highly visible three-inch scab for days and then a white scar followed which stood out in contrast with my deep summer tan. I was angry that I had to stay out of the water for a week so that the salty ocean water wouldn't dissolve the scab and slow the healing. Dallas noted that he'd not seen Louise at the waterfront. I'd guessed she felt too guilty to see me.

Dallas and I kicked off our track meet with grand results which pleased Major Axelrod, the camp director. The mile run saw three of our campers come in around five minutes and four came in under twelve seconds in the 100-yard dash. One of the senior boys won the long jump with a leap of 21 feet, and two of our competitors cleared six feet in the high jump. There was some real talent in our camp. Awards and medals were given at a special dinner a week later.

Summer was now drawing rapidly toward the end of August. John English invited me and Dallas to join him for a mixer at Phil Rigby's house. I had sworn I'd never touch another drop of gin. Just the smell of it made me sick. But over the summer, I had acquired a taste for beer, usually never more than two cans or bottles and never drinking to the hated stage of drunkenness. English, himself a beer drinker, said there'd be plenty of Schlitz, as well as cool snacks at the mixer. Rigby was a generous host. I did have the thought that Rigby could get himself into a load of trouble for providing minors with alcohol. But in those days, it was a common occurrence at intimate house parties. I still resented the fact that Rigby hadn't stepped up and stopped me drinking earlier that summer which I'm sure caused me to have some alcohol poisoning. What if I had been hospitalized or had died?

The Kingston Trio was playing on the stereo when we arrived at the Rigby mixer. There was a dozen or so people milling about with cocktails in one hand and most people with a cigarette in the other. Thank God, I hadn't been attracted to that awful habit. I valued my wind. English seemed familiar with most of the people and especially with Rigby with whom he was an old pal. Half the people were older women in their mid to late twenties, cosmopolitan, dark-eyed with heavy makeup, form-fitting skirts, and alluring perfume. Rigby led me and Dallas to the bar and snapped open a couple tall cans of Schlitz beer for us. I felt a bit lost in the environment and so was Dallas. But then one of the pretty older women approached and engaged Dallas in a conversation, asking him if he played football and for whom. I was sure she'd been clued in by Rigby. Dallas launched into telling her about his football laurels and scholarship offers.

I excused myself and wandered out onto the front deck of the smart house where one could gaze at the panorama of the early evening Pacific. The marshy cove below had a couple lithe Egrets picking their way with slow tentative steps through the shallows. Then I saw Louise below coming to the house and up the walk to the front door. She couldn't see me above. I wasn't sure about seeing her or how to talk to her. I had mixed feelings. I was also questioning what she was doing by coming to this very adult-like party. She must have been invited.

After finishing my can of Schlitz, my courage a bit bolstered, I went back into the house and saw Louise mixing. She was chic in a clinging powder blue sheath and much taller than I had remembered, now wearing shiny black stilettos. As soon as she saw me, she broke off chatting with an older man about Rigby's age and came toward me, elegantly holding her half-drunk Martini glass.

"I didn't know you knew Phil Rigby," I said before she could speak.

"I met him a couple years ago. I mean, my family's house is only two streets over from here." We were both acting matter-of-factly, restraining any show of feelings.

"How's the scratch?" she said, softening her expression.

"It's healed. How about your acceptance to UCLA?"

"Done. I'm in. I also got admitted into a very promising new clinical trial."

I wondered if she was still in remission. Cancer was something they could never predict. But I didn't broach the topic and she said she was fine and was starting off with ten easy units of lower division classes rather than the usual sixteen.

"Keeping the stress at a minimum, you know."

She had that same wave of long hair hanging down on her right side that gave some cover to a matching powder blue eye patch. She looked very mature and sexy in her sleek evening dress and her smile was as sweet as her perfume. Guilt and forgiveness flooded my heart and the aching pity I had once felt came back to me. She was so beautiful yet so awfully fragile and vulnerable. The scratch was an accident and just a scratch after all.

ACKNOWLEDGMENT

To novelist Dan Armstrong, for his inestimable help in proofreading and editing this book.

Made in United States
North Haven, CT
10 March 2024